Best Wishes
CJ Dalton

My Heart is my Own

WILLIAM T. ROTH III —
ATTORNEY AT LAW

by

C.J. Dalton

AuthorHouse™
1663 Liberty Drive, Suite 200
Bloomington, IN 47403
www.authorhouse.com
Phone: 1-800-839-8640

First published by AuthorHouse 11/14/2007

ISBN: 978-1-4343-3345-2 (sc)

Printed in the United States of America
Bloomington, Indiana

This book is printed on acid-free paper.

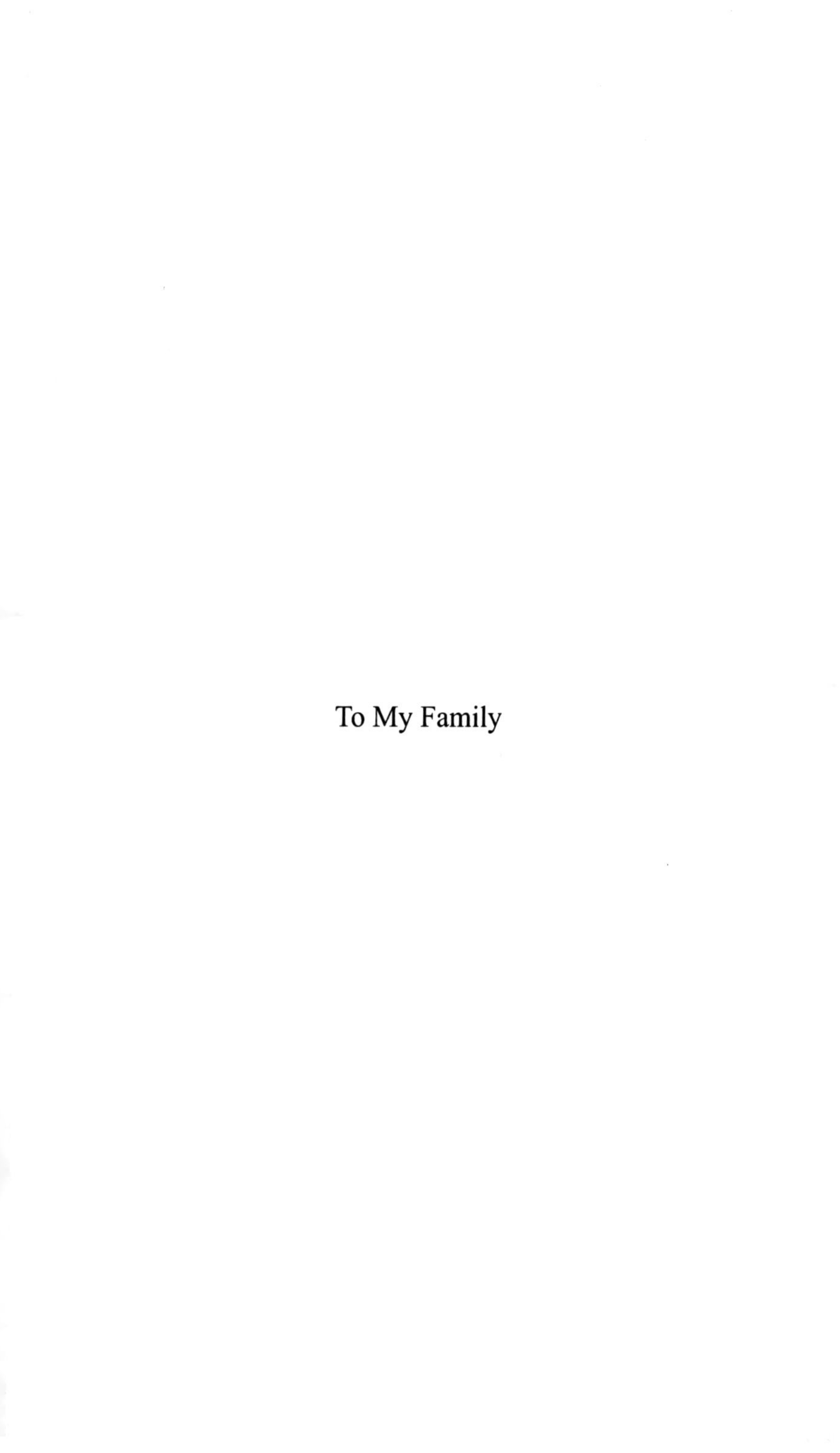

To My Family

It was a rainy Monday morning in a Southern Middle Tennessee town. The rain had slowed just enough for Bill Roth to walk from his law office across the street to the court house, which he did regularly to present cases before the county judge. Bill was in the habit of having a cup of coffee before he walked over, but this morning he was in a hurry because he needed to speak with his client before walking into the courtroom. This morning there would be a jury present, and he knew he had his work cut out for him.

This case involved a local man, Tom Wilson, who had been severely injured in an industrial accident at a large local plant. The man had received damage to both legs and arms. Bill had worked on preparing this case for months. He felt that he was completely prepared, and he knew that his client should receive much compensation for his injuries and mental anguish. He had to convince the jury of this too. Bill was well known in town for his brilliance in law and his ability to argue cases to the nth degree. He was very self-confident and polished. He was also a handsome man with a kind and pleasing personality and was very distinct in speech and presentation.

On this particular day, he was dressed in a navy pin-striped suit, a pale blue shirt, and muted tie. His graying hair and beard were trimmed to perfection, and his piercing brown eyes were wide and dancing.

As he entered the courtroom, his client joined him. They shook hands, and Bill ushered him down the aisle, to the front of the court room. They sat down in two chairs at a table as twelve jury members filed in and took their seats. Bill had already prepared to question the jury, so he stood and began to ask his series of questions to the first juror. He went slowly and questioned each juror one at a time. As he finished, he sat down beside his client, and the plaintiff's attorney followed suit. When both attorneys were satisfied that this was a competent jury, the trial began. Bill called witnesses to testify in his client's behalf. After several witnesses had testified, it was close to eleven o'clock, so the judge called a recess for lunch.

The rain had stopped now, and the sun was out. Bill and his client walked back to his office, where he sent out for their lunch. Bill made a phone call to his friend Zoa Britton as he sat at his desk. He asked her to have dinner with him at six o'clock. He told her that he would be over as soon as he was finished for the day. As he hung up the phone, their food arrived, so he and Tom Wilson sat and talked as they ate. Bill told him that he felt things were going well, and he planned to bring him to the witness stand later in the day. He was confident that this would be a short trial and would be settled quickly. As their lunch break ended, Bill and Tom walked back to the courthouse. The jury had returned, and as the judge walked in, the court was called into session and the trial continued.

The plaintiff's witnesses were called to the stand. Pictures were passed around to the jury, and doctors' reports were read. Bill called Tom Wilson to the stand. As he was questioned, he became very emotional, and wept. The jury could see that he was severely shaken as he told about the accident and what he remembered of that day. He told of his injuries and how this would affect his family. Bill knew that this testimony would probably cinch their case. He felt that the jury understood that the company responsible for this accident must pay.

The attorney for the plaintiff gave his summation, and Bill began his closing remarks. He was very precise and spoke with authority in a quiet voice as he asked for compensation for his client who had suffered so much physical and emotional trauma.

His closing remarks ended, and the judge gave instructions to the jury. The jury filed into the jury room. Bill and Tom Wilson sat and waited. The jury was out for only an hour before they returned with a verdict. The jury foreman read the jurors' statement. Tom Wilson would receive one million dollars for his injuries, a lifetime of compensation from his insurance coverage, fifty thousand dollars because he could no longer work, and a twenty thousand dollar compensation for his family.

The judge stood and thanked the jury for their fairness, and the court was called out of session by the court officer. Bill shook hands with Tom as they both grinned with happiness and relief. This litigation had lasted for four years, and Bill was relieved for both of them that it was over.

They returned to Bill's office and talked for a while. Bill explained to Tom how and when he would receive the money. Tom left the office to go home, and Bill sat down and finally enjoyed the cup of coffee he had missed this morning. He tried to relax as he thought back over the day. He just needed to sit here for a while and "chill out" before he drove to his condo for a shower and a change of clothes, then picked Zoa up for dinner.

He thought of her now for the first time since he had talked to her at lunch. Zoa—how did she feel about him, and how did he feel about her? They had been friends for only a couple of months now.

As her image came to his mind, he could feel the warmth of her wrap around him. He could hardly wait to see her. He really wanted them to be more than friends, but with his practice, he wondered how he could give himself to a committed relationship. He had been married before, but it hadn't worked out. He'd had to spend too much time working on legal documents, and more time in other towns in court. The marriage hadn't work, and so it had ended.

His ex-wife Christie's image came to his mind now—the good times and the bad, and the final days of their marriage. He had made the decision to end it himself, and had moved out of their house while she had been out of town with her family. What a cowardly thing for him to do, but he felt it had been best for both of them. That had been a little over two years ago. Even though he was very busy, he had been alone, and lonely, and then one day a couple of months ago, he met Zoa Britton.

He was in another town for a trial that day, and after a taxing day he decided to go by the mall on his way home. He needed to pick up some shirts and ties for himself. He bought the items he needed, rode down on the escalator to the main floor, and stopped at the men's fragrance counter.

He was sampling a fragrance when a very pretty young woman with flashing brown eyes and a fantastic smile greeted him and asked if she could be of assistance. For some reason, probably because of his loneliness, a chill ran over his body, and for a brief second he thought he was becoming ill. He just stood there and looked at her. Then he said, "Yes, I think maybe you can help me. I am trying to find a new fragrance, something different." She immediately began to help him find something. She spoke so softly, with much knowledge about the products. He searched her hand with his eyes for a wedding ring. There was none. He decided on a cologne and a shower gel and paid for them with his credit card. He wanted to find out some things about this pretty girl, but before he could say anything, she asked, "Are you a doctor, or a business executive?" "No," he said. "I'm an attorney." They both laughed. The conversation flowed between them, and before he left the store, he had her phone number. He called her a few days later, and they had gone out a lot since then. Every time he was with her, it was like that first time; the chills ran over him profusely.

Bill finished the cup of coffee he was drinking, straightened his desk, and filed papers from today's trial. He filled his briefcase with papers and notebooks for tomorrow's trial, got his laptop, slipped into his suit jacket, turned out the lights in his office, locked the door, and walked to his Ranger parked in the office parking lot. It was still daylight outside, and the sun was bright as he drove home. He put a CD in the player and relaxed as he drove. He turned into his driveway a short while later and parked the Ranger around back. He got his briefcase and laptop out of the back, unlocked his door, and went inside.

He was so very glad to be home. He went into the bedroom, took his suit coat, tie, and shirt and trousers off and hung them in his closet. He reached for a short terry robe and put it on and then laid out a nice sports shirt, pants, and jacket for tonight. He went into his large bathroom and turned on the water in the Jacuzzi. Tonight he needed more than a shower to relax his tense body. He had some extra time to relax, so he strolled back into the kitchen, opened the refrigerator, and poured himself a glass of wine. By the time he returned to the bathroom, the Jacuzzi was filled and the jets were churning. He removed his robe and shorts and slid into the wonderful tepid water.

All of the cares of the day slipped away as he lay back and let his body completely relax. He listened to a CD, closed his eyes, and thought of Zoa. He wondered how tonight would end. He really wanted and needed to go to bed with her, but he knew that he would want to stay the night with her, and he had the trial tomorrow at nine. He realized that his practice had become his life and that he must find a way to enjoy the relationships he pursued. He needed the passion of love just as well as the passion of his work to fulfill his needs. So he would have to find a happy medium.

He got out of the tub, dried himself off, and dressed in the clothes he had laid out earlier. He looked at himself in the mirror and felt good about what he saw.

Zoa was ready and waiting when Bill arrived. She was dressed in a black pantsuit and wore her honey blond hair pulled back with a crystal barrette. She so much looked forward to being with Bill Roth. He was becoming a very special part of her life, but she knew better than to fall too hard because she knew that his practice was the major part of his life. She wanted them to take it slow, have fun together, and enjoy each other. She knew Bill had been married previously, even though he seldom spoke of his marriage. Tonight she hoped that she could relieve him of some of the stress he seemed to carry.

Bill arrived at Zoa's apartment and rang the door bell. She opened the door for him and invited him inside. Bill meant to be "cool," but he was so drawn to Zoa that he could not stop himself from taking her in his arms and kissing her slowly and with passion. She responded to him and returned his kiss. He regained his composure and asked, "Are you ready to go for dinner?" She replied, "Bill I can make dinner, and we can stay here if you want." Bill thought for what seemed like an eternity, but then said, "No, I want us to go out, and besides, I've made reservations for us." They looked at each other, and at once they both knew that neither of them felt hunger for food.

What they both wanted more for the rest of the night was to be together, and make love over and over.

She reached for his hand and led him down the hall to her bedroom. For the rest of the night until early dawn, they were together—body to body, soul to soul, and Bill never felt so good in his life.

Somewhere around four a.m., Bill's thoughts brought him back to reality. WOW! He had a trial at nine in another town. Duh-uh—his brain clicked! He kissed Zoa very gently and rose to shower and leave. He knew he had to be alert and on his toes. He told Zoa, "Last night was awesome. I just meant for us to go out and enjoy a nice dinner. I didn't expect this to happen, it just did." "I know," she said as she kissed him. "I'm not sorry about last night. I loved it. Bill, it was wonderful. I wish you could stay, but I do understand. Bill, please don't let all the tomorrows of your life be work. You deserve happiness with whomever you choose. I've come to love these times we've spent together for these two months. I hope there'll be many more times like last night." Bill kissed her once more and went to shower and dress. In his heart he knew that he just could not be committed to one woman again, at least not now. As he left, he told Zoa he would call her soon.

He was on his way home, and it was close to six o'clock. He decided to drive by Hardee's and picked up his breakfast. He drove through and ordered a sausage and egg biscuit, sweet roll, and hot coffee. His condo was only a couple of blocks away, so he took the bag with his food and drove home. He would go over the notes on his laptop for the trial later. He also had to lay out clothes and dress. All of his thoughts were on the day ahead. He tried not to let last night with Zoa creep into his mind.

Bill arrived back at his condo. He felt so rejuvenated and relaxed. He wished he had time to throw on some sweats and run a few blocks—he felt that good, but he had to go over the trial notes and get everything in his mind before court. So he unlocked the door and went inside, took off his clothes, and put his terry robe back on. He sat down at the kitchen table and opened the Hardee's sack. He was so hungry. He realized that he hadn't eaten since lunch yesterday. He devoured the sausage biscuit and drank the coffee, which by now was lukewarm. He decided to make a pot of coffee to try to wake himself up. When it was ready, he poured a cup and ate the sweet roll. He got his laptop, set it on the table, and pulled up the notes for today's trial. He had worked on this case for a few weeks, and was confident and familiar with the material. It was not unusual for him to be working on several cases at once. Last night had caught him off-guard, though, and it was a little harder for him to get himself focused this morning. He felt giddy inside, warm and satisfied. He knew that having sex with Zoa had made him feel this way. He needed it more often, but there was something about Zoa that engulfed him. He just could not fall in love. He had met so many different women in his profession, some of them attorneys, who were so incredibly seductive. He could have most any one he desired, but Zoa made him feel so warm. There was something about her that just overwhelmed him. He had to somehow forget last night for a while.

He left his laptop and went to his bedroom to get dressed. He chose a black suit, white shirt, and floral tie. It was now seven thirty. He knew that traffic would be heavy this morning as he drove to the nearby town. He got his laptop, his notes, and legal pads together. He forgot that he hadn't brushed his teeth, so he ran and took care of that—and was on his way.

The traffic to Springfield, a small town west, was not as heavy as Bill had thought it would be this early in the morning. He was giving himself plenty of time just in case. He drove his Ford Ranger with ease along the interstate. He would meet his clients in plenty of time before the trial began. He felt good and knew that today would be a great day. After last night, and this morning, how could it be otherwise? His mind drifted back to Zoa. The night with her had satisfied his very being. He didn't think he could not see her again, which was what he was trying to convince himself to do. He was so afraid to fall in love. It couldn't be love he felt—it was just the most fabulous sex he had had in a long time, and it beckoned him to return.

He arrived at the courthouse in the country town of Springfield at eight thirty. Court began at nine o'clock. His clients were waiting inside for him. Their names were Doris and Paul Bell, and their case concerned an automobile accident that had happened six months earlier. The Bells, a very nice couple in their mid-seventies, had been injured—not severely, but the accident had left them so traumatically scarred that neither could drive a car anymore. Their children now had to help them. They had been hit in the rear by a young woman who simply had not been paying attention. She had been talking on a cell phone.

The young woman, Bethany Caldwell, was an employee at a bank in town. She was a pretty, tall, slender brunette. The attorney representing her was John Todd, a local attorney whom Bill knew well. They had attended law school together, and both were about the same age, mid-forties. John Todd was a fine attorney, and Bill knew he would represent his client well. Bill also knew that the jury would most likely favor his clients, since Miss Caldwell had been distracted by the cell phone and had plowed into the Bells' car from the rear. Their car was a total loss, and both of the Bells had been bruised and battered by the collision and emotionally scarred. Bill hoped and felt that he could get the Bells a nice compensation for their injuries. He had worked cases like this many times, and you could never tell exactly how the jury would react, but he planned to give it his best shot. He had all the information and data he needed and had confidence that he could present it well.

Bill and the Bells took their seats on one side of the court room. John Todd and his client, Bethany Caldwell, sat on the other side. The selected jury, seven women and five men, filed in and took their seats. The judge, Charles Thomas, walked in and the court officer announced, "All rise." The trial began.

Bill rose and began to question a witness to the accident. According to the first witness, he was traveling two cars behind the Bells and one car behind Beth Caldwell when he had to break suddenly to avoid being involved in the accident. He told Bill and the jury that the Bells were driving normally and that Miss Caldwell suddenly crashed into them from the rear, never braking her car. It seemed that she must have been distracted in some way.

He had pulled his car to the side of the road to call 911 on his cell phone to get help for the accident victims and then walked over to the cars to see if he could give assistance. He said when he got to the cars, both were heavily damaged, but Miss Caldwell was standing outside her car and did not appear to be injured. The Bells were still in their seats and seemed to be in shock. Mrs. Bell was complaining of pain and was crying. Mr. Bell had some cuts and bruises on his face and asked the witness to please help them. The witness told them that help was on the way. He said that he stayed by the cars, consoling the Bells until an ambulance arrived, and he told the police what he had seen. Miss Caldwell also stayed there and seemed to cooperate with the authorities. She told them that she simply hadn't been paying attention and had been talking on her cell phone. She was very remorseful at the scene, he said. Bill thanked the witness, and John Todd began to question him.

Bill sat down and listened, taking notes as he sat there. As soon as John Todd finished questioning the witness, the judge called a recess for lunch. The Bells left for lunch with their son. Bill decided to go to a nearby tea room where he ate occasionally when he was in town. He needed to relax a few minutes, and he wanted to be alone. He took his briefcase and sat at a table in a room by himself. He ordered lunch, and while he waited, he opened his briefcase to go over some notes. As he did, he saw a pink handwritten Post-it note on top of his legal pad. He unfolded it and read the message: "Hi——You are So Handsome. Call Me—768-6991."

Don't judge me too harshly, Beth! For heaven's sake, how did this get in his briefcase, and why would she do this? Where had he been so lax that someone could have access to his notes? Oh boy! Nothing like this had ever happened to him before in his entire career. Last night had certainly left him dazed, but he had tried to gain control. Right now everything seemed out of control. He could do lots of things with the note, but he wasn't going to even consider it. He was going to eat his lunch, go back to court, and win this case for the Bells. He would be focused and alert. His lunch was wonderful. He felt refreshed and headed back to the court room, ready for battle.

The judge called Miss Caldwell to the stand first. Thank goodness John Todd would question her first. Even though Bill was composed, he could not look at Bethany Caldwell without wondering how on earth she was able to get that note in his briefcase, And why she would attempt such a stunt. He watched her closely as John Todd questioned her, and tried to recall in his mind if he had seen this girl before—but no, he knew that he had not.

John Todd finished his questions and sat down. It was Bill's turn. He stood in front of Beth Caldwell so that he could look directly into her eyes. She did not look directly at him and had no expression on her face. He questioned her about her job, and how long she had worked at the bank, and why she had been in such a hurry on the morning of the accident.

She told him that she was not exceeding the speed limit but that she simply was not paying attention as she talked on the phone. She said, "I'm so sorry for my recklessness."

Bill said, "Thank you. That will be all, your honor." He knew that she was remorseful and accepted responsibility for her actions. The jury would consider all of this in their settlement of the case. Beth Caldwell had good insurance. It would all be taken care of. He also knew that he would hear from Miss Caldwell again. He would not call the number on the pink Post-it note, and he would definitely tear it up—shred it, actually. But she would call him after this trial was over—one day soon.

The jury was out about thirty minutes. The Bells received one hundred fifty thousand dollars. Everyone seemed happy and relieved that the trial was over. Bill talked with the Bells and told them that he would be in touch with them as soon as the settlement was made. He saw Bethany Caldwell leave the court room with her attorney. He hoped that she did not mention the note to him. He almost knew that she would not. Bill went to his Ranger and was glad to be on his way home. He needed to stop by his office, but just to relax and drive would help his nerves. This day had definitely gotten to him. He picked up his cell phone to call Zoa but hung up and dialed his secretary to see what had gone on at the office today. He knew that he had to stay focused on his practice—his life.

Betty Davis, Bill's secretary, answered the phone on the second ring. "Hi!" he said, "how are you?" "What's going on?" Betty was used to her boss's calls during the day, and she was always happy to hear his voice. She could tell that he was tired today and kind of stressed out.

"I'm fine," she answered," but you sound a bit spent."

"Yes, you got it. Not a good day. I thought if there wasn't anything I needed to sign, or calls to return, I might go on home."

"No, boss," she replied. "I've taken care of everything. It's been a slow day."

"Okay," Bill told her, "I'll see you tomorrow, and thank goodness it's Friday."

"Bill, why don't you take the weekend off and go somewhere fun and relax?"

"Think I need to get away, do you?" Bill asked.

"I think you and I need to talk soon, Bill."

"Okay, Betty, I'll take your advice for once. I'm exhausted and I just want to go home and collapse. I'll grab a bite to eat, and I may or may not see you tomorrow, but I will check in."

"Goodnight, boss," she said.

Betty hung up as she thought of Bill. She had a wee crush on him herself, but she knew it would never work, as he saw her only as his right hand. She was at least five years older, and not his type, she thought, anyway. Bill was strictly business. No fun and games; she felt like a "true professional." She felt it could be interesting to change that, but for now she would just remain his right hand. It seemed to be what he wanted. She would be there for him.

Bill stopped for a sub sandwich and a Coke and headed on home. He planned to eat, take a shower, and go to bed. He had nothing else on his mind at the time. The phone was ringing as he unlocked his front door. He checked the caller ID and saw that it was Zoa. Even though he was exhausted, he answered.

"Hi," she said in a whisper. "I had you on my mind and just wanted to see how you were, and how today went."

"I'm glad you called," Bill grinned. " I really needed to hear your voice. Today has been a difficult day and I'm spent. This day got to me. How are you, and how has your day been? I thought of you, and last night, a lot today."

"Last night was fantastic. Bill, come back over tonight and we'll repeat it. I miss you, and I want you."

"Tell you what, I'm so exhausted, I've got to get some sleep, but let's talk tomorrow. I'd like for us to spend the weekend somewhere. Think about where you'd like to go, and we'll leave early in the afternoon and stay until Sunday. I don't have any appointments tomorrow, so I'll be free by two o'clock. We could drive to Gatlinburg, down to Memphis, or over to the lake in Kentucky. There's a nice cabin we could stay in and enjoy the lake and nature. Those are a few suggestions. I'll let you decide."

"Bill, it sounds wonderful. "We'll talk tomorrow. Get some rest now, and I'll talk to you later."

"Hey, you aren't mad, are you?" he asked.

"No, I'm not mad. I just really wanted to be with you tonight. I don't want to sound pathetic."

"Zoa, listen to me, pack a bag, get in your car and drive over here. I'll be waiting. I'll fill the Jacuzzi, put on a CD, light some candles, and I promise, it'll be worth your drive. We'll go from there with plans for the weekend. I want you to come, Zoa. Chill out with me, will you?

"Yes, Bill, I'll be there within two hours. Bye."

When he hung up, Bill wished that he hadn't answered the phone. He wanted to be with Zoa, but tonight was not a good night. His mind was tired, and his body was exhausted, but he'd heard the disappointment in Zoas' voice. He would have to revive himself somehow, and get ready fast.

He went to the fridge and poured himself a glass of wine. Its warmth gave his body a lift as he swallowed it. He had cheese in the fridge, so he sliced some and put it between crackers. The sub sandwich had to be forgotten for now.

He put a bottle of champagne on ice, then turned the water on to fill the hot tub. He got in the shower and washed his body with the delicious smelling shower gel he had purchased from Zoa a while back. This revived his body quickly, and he felt himself coming to life again. He dressed in sweats and lit some candles all around the hot tub. His anticipation was now mounting. Zoa was prepared to leave home to go to Bill's.

In the times they had dated, she had never been there. She wished she had not called him tonight. She realized it was not a good time, but she so much wanted to see him and be with him. In the future she would not be so forward. He seemed aloof, but warm to her, but she knew that it was he who would take the lead, if there was to be a relationship. She knew already that she loved Bill Roth, but she had to back off and play it cool. If they did go away for the weekend, she would get as close to Bill as she could get. She packed her bag with clothes that she thought he would like on her, dressed in a pink jogging suit and sandals, locked the door, got in her black Mustang convertible, and headed to Bill's condo.

While Bill lay on his bed and waited for Zoa, he thought about his life, how he had always been determined to be the best attorney he could be, and he had achieved that goal. Since law school he had worked and worked to be the best. He had had little time for much else. He had also wanted a wife and a family, but it hadn't worked out. He had met Christy when he had still been in law school. He loved her, he'd thought. They had had some very good times together and shared many interests, but as his practice had grown, they'd drifted apart. They'd become more like friends and definitely not lovers anymore. Christy had begun to let herself go, putting on weight and not paying much attention to their home. He had focused on his career and how he looked. He had run when he could, keeping himself in shape, and had bought nice clothes. He had begun to notice young, pretty female attorneys in court, who had made passes at him, and some had even asked him out, but he'd never cheated on Christy. He had just begun to pull away, and more and more he had found excuses to work.

One day while she had been out of town, he'd packed his bags, chosen a few pieces of furniture, and moved into this condo. It hadn't been good for his image, but he'd filed for divorce. Christy had not contested. He hadn't liked himself afterward for what he had done. He had been lonely, but he had kept focused on his work; and then one day a while back, he had met Zoa. He loved being with her, and they seemed to be getting closer, but he was afraid—afraid he would fall in love. He just could not commit himself again so soon. He had hurt Zoa already, but she was coming over anyway. He would make tonight as special as he could for her.

Zoa arrived at Bill's condo. She didn't know what to expect, but when she saw the neighborhood, she knew that his home would be lovely. She rang the bell, and Bill answered, smiling and so excited to see her. He took her bag, closed the door, and opened his arms as she came to him. He kissed her slowly and felt her give to him as if she couldn't get enough. He asked her if she wanted to get in the Jacuzzi. She told him that she was here to make love to him now. "Come with me," he said, as he led her upstairs to his king-size bed.

He kissed Zoa hard and touched her face and neck, unbuttoned her blouse, held her breasts, and kissed them. He was so aroused he tore at his clothes and threw them on the floor as she undressed. He wanted her so much he could not stand to wait. Neither could she. She lay on the bed and pulled him down to her as he kissed her mouth and then her breasts. As they kissed long and hard, she touched and tugged at him. Their passion pulled them together, and they both reached a height beyond their control. It was so satisfying and consuming that they could not move for a long time. Zoa lay in Bill's arms all night.

Bill awoke at dawn. Zoa was still sleeping soundly. He rose, pulled on a robe, and went to shower. He was used to rising early. It was his life and his way. The hot steamy water and the shower gel cleansed not only his body, but his mind, and his spirit. Last night and the night before had satisfied him so immensely. He was restless somehow, though, as if he shouldn't be here with Zoa like this. He didn't understand why he felt this way. He couldn't shake the feeling. He stayed in the shower a long time, until he smelled the aroma of coffee brewing and bacon and eggs cooking.

Zoa must have awoken and was preparing breakfast for them. He dried himself off, slipped into his robe, and went into the kitchen. Zoa, wearing a very sexy robe, was making breakfast. She had the table set and the food ready. When he saw her, he became so aroused he forgot the feeling that he'd had earlier. He walked over and took her in his arms and kissed her again so passionately.

"WOW!"

She laughed. " I guess you aren't hungry for this food I've fixed."

"I am hungry," he said. "Starved for you."

She said, "We'll have time for that later. I want you to eat. There's no telling when you ate last."

"I can't remember," he said.

Together they sat at the table and ate breakfast. Bill drank two cups of coffee and ate a cinnamon roll besides the bacon, eggs, and buttered toast. He was famished.

"I told you you needed food," Zoa said.

"I guess you were right. I didn't realize how hungry I was. Zoa, I need to go down to the office and check in, see what's going on this morning. You can stay here if you wish. I hope to be out of there by two o'clock. If you want us to get away, we can leave when I get home. We can call and make reservations, or we can stay here and chill out for the weekend.

Zoa felt that she was going to cry. Bill had hurt her last night when she'd called to check on him and he'd said he was tired and couldn't come over, but she had packed a bag and come to him when he'd asked her. They'd had incredible sex, and she'd thought he planned to stay with her today, repeating last night all day, and then they would go away for the weekend together. Now he said he was going to the office, would be there until two, and she could stay here if she wished. She had let herself fall too hard for Bill. She saw it now and knew she had to back off.

"Bill," she said, fighting back tears, "I don't think I can go away for the weekend. I need to take care of some business I've put off for a while. I'll get my things together and leave after I've put things in order here in the kitchen. Perhaps another time. You go on to work. We'll talk later."

Realizing that he had hurt her again, Bill saw that this came from the feelings he had had earlier, so he had to straighten it out now. He would deal with his feelings later. He walked over to Zoa and put his hands on her face. "You are so lovely," he said, "so kind, so gentle, and so exciting, so loving, so sexy. You have satisfied my very being. I have never felt so drawn to anyone, or so complete—and yet I'm afraid I'll hurt you. I can't give myself to this relationship right now, Zoa. I can't say 'I love you' at this moment. I need time."

"Bill, take all the time you need. Please know that I love you already, and I don't need time, but I want to stay away until you know what you want."

She went to shower. Bill dressed and left to drive to his office. He knew that he would have to deal with this real soon. Right now he preferred to concentrate on his work.

He parked his Ranger and walked into his office. He buzzed Betty and let her know he was in. "I'm surprised, boss," she said. "I thought you were probably 'sleeping in' this morning."

"You knew I couldn't stay away, didn't you?"

"There's donuts and coffee. How about if I bring you a chocolate donut and a cup of hot coffee?"

"You know I can't resist that Betty, and thanks. Also, let's talk. I want to know what's going on. You can fill me in. Bring yourself a cup and join me."

"I'll be there shortly," she said.

Bill hung up the phone, took his jacket off, opened his briefcase, and plugged in his laptop. He pulled up notes for his next case and was reading when Betty knocked. She had a lovely tray, complete with a red rosebud vase, their coffee, his donut, and pretty flowered napkins. "Hey, thanks, this is a bright opener for my day," he said. She could see that Bill was distracted this morning, but she didn't dare ask questions. "Sit down, Betty," he said, "and talk to me. Tell me what's going on. Any calls? Matters of urgency?"

"Routine papers to sign, and you have an appointment at ten to draw up a will for Judy and Bill Connor. Nothing that's really pressing. Oh yes, you had a phone call from a Miss Caldwell . . . said she would call back later." Bill had been expecting that call, but he didn't say anything.

"I'm planning to stay all day, Betty, so I'll be available for calls, and even an appointment or two."

"Okay, boss," she replied. "Anything else?" They drank their coffee and sat in silence for a few minutes. Bill looked directly into her eyes as he seldom did, and she could see the sadness there.

"Boss, what is it? Am I being too intuitive to ask, are you okay?"

"Betty, I need to talk to you strictly confidential, and I need your advice."

"Good," she said. "I told you the other day we needed to talk."

"You know already, I think, that I have been dating Zoa Britton, even though I haven't introduced her around. I've been seeing her a couple of months or so. I met her one day a while back when I stopped at the mall to buy some shirts. She works at Dillard's there. She's a lovely person, and I've found myself responding to her immensely. Except, Betty, I have this fear within—I really don't know what it is—like this isn't right, like I can't have another relationship without hurting someone or getting hurt, or both. I've already hurt her, I know, in the last two days because I just froze. I used the excuse of being too tired to go see her, and today the excuse of coming in to work and leaving her at my house. Give me some advice, Betty—you are my right hand, and you're wise."

Betty had listened very intently, and in her heart she wanted to say, "Let me help you get over her," but she couldn't and wouldn't do that. "Boss, I have never pried in your life. I knew that if and when you wanted to tell me anything confidential, you would do so. I watch you work so hard and remain so devoted to your profession, and I think to myself, he so needs some R&R, and someone to enjoy it with. I didn't know that you were seeing someone special, but I doubted you were entirely celibate." She grinned as she said, "You are a handsome, successful attorney, and no one could help but notice that. I think that you haven't entirely gotten over your divorce. You've buried yourself in your work, but you haven't dealt with your feelings. Maybe you don't want to have a serious relationship now or maybe never, but you must deal with those feelings. You can't just hide them inside."

"Betty, I don't think I'm in love with Zoa. She is fabulous, and I don't mind saying, she satisfies my very being, more than Christy ever did, and I thought I loved her. I wanted our marriage to last, and I wanted a family, but Christy and I weren't alike. I saw that after a while. Zoa seems different, and she says, 'I love you Bill, I don't need time to think about it.' We both agreed to stay apart and see how we feel. I'm going to continue to focus on work. It keeps me going, and it's my life. If it's meant for Zoa and I to be together, it will happen. If not, maybe there's someone else out there."

"You can have anyone you want, boss, but there *is* someone out there for you, and I believe you will find that someone if you really want her, and she you." How Betty longed to tell Bill that she would love to be that someone. He hadn't the slightest, though, and that was best for now. "Bill," she said, "if there is anything I can do for you, or if you need to talk anytime, I am here, or at home, and I'm always free to talk or listen. You know I'm alone, so call if you need to."

"Thanks, Betty, for being here and being you. Now I guess its time for us to get busy," he said. Betty picked up their cups and saucers and napkins and put them on the tray. She left the red rose on his desk, and walked back to her office. He got busy at his computer and was lost in his next case when Betty buzzed him and said, "Miss Caldwell is on the phone."

Dear God, he had hoped she wouldn't call back. What was he going to say?—how to handle this? "Bill Roth," he answered in a very businesslike voice.

"Hi," she said. "I guess you remember me."

"Yes, I do," he said. "Why are you calling me?"

"You got my note, didn't you?"

"That note could have gotten you and me in a lot of trouble if I had not destroyed it."

"But you did, and that tells me something. Look, Bill, the trial is over. I took responsibility for what I did, and will pay. I lost my job, and my car is demolished. Thank goodness I had good insurance to cover the Bells, but I have to hunt another job. I told you in the note—I find you very attractive. I would like to meet you, say for lunch or dinner, and get to know you. I believe we have some things in common."

"You don't know me, Miss Caldwell, and you are very forward, first of all by taking the chance of getting that note in my briefcase. I won't even ask how you accomplished that, and now you call my office and ask me to meet you."

"Will you?"

"No, I can't and won't do that."

"You haven't said you don't want to."

"I'm saying it now. I don't want to, and I am not."

"Look, Bill, I need to talk to you. You seem so understanding and kind."

"You have your attorney. Talk to him. He will help you if you need help."

"Bill, I want to be with you. I felt it the minute I saw you. I could satisfy you and make you happy."

"This conversation is over. Please do not call me again. This office is for business only. Don't call again."

Bill hung up and buzzed Betty. "Don't take any more calls from Miss Caldwell. Hang up if she persists."

"Sure, boss. By the way, the Connors are here to write their will."

"Betty, give me about five minutes and send them in. Okay? Thanks."

Bill stood and stretched, trying to relieve some of the tension he felt. He walked over to the window and looked outside. The sunshine was bright. It was a wonderful day. He hoped that he could put his life in some kind of order. He thought of his talk with Betty earlier. She had said that she would be there for him. Hadn't she always been there? She knew all about the office and could run it herself if she needed to. She had had paralegal training and was only a short step away from becoming an attorney. She was attractive to—not beautiful like Zoa, but pretty and kind, and she had an understanding heart. She found him attractive too, by her comments earlier. Would it be kosher to ask his secretary out? He thought it would be great for them to have dinner together. He would ask her later.

He walked to the front office and greeted Bill and Judy Connors and asked them to come into his office. Bill had known the Connors a long time and had helped them with legal work on many occasions. They talked together for a while before he started to write their will. Bill Connors said, "Bill, as you know, Judy and I don't have any children. Matter of fact, all of our family has passed away. We want to leave what we have to you, Bill, after we're gone. Of course, we want to be sure that you will accept our gift and will take care of everything for us. We'll list for you all of our holdings, which are substantial, including our home here in town, a beach home in Fort Myers, Florida, and a chateau in Gatlinburg, Tennessee. There is a large amount of stock in Con Ed and GE, and a few CDs and savings accounts. In other words, Bill, you will be a very wealthy man one day. Judy and I are older but we seem to be in good health. One never knows, but one should be prepared in case."

Bill had been listening intently as his friend spoke. He felt so humble, and really in shock, even though he did look and act calm and grateful. He spoke to Bill and Judy in his kindest voice, with some emotion. "I am overwhelmed," he said, "speechless. In all my years in law, I have never received such a generous gift. I cannot begin to thank you both. Now, I'll write this as you tell me. We'll get it all together, I'll read it over, and then my secretary will type it up. You both can sign it, and either she or I will notarize it. I'll take care of everything for you. You won't have to worry."

Bill took out his legal pad and began to write as the Connors dictated their wishes and listed their assets. Bill Connors said, "Bill, I know that you are well-off yourself. You probably don't really need our wealth, but we think of you as 'our son,' a close mentor and friend. You have been so good to us, always helping us and giving us legal advice for free. I know that in whatever capacity you use our assets, it will be for good." Bill thanked the Connors again. They sat and talked for close to an hour. Bill told them that he would get everything typed and notarized and then would call them to come back in and sign the will, probably on Monday. They shook hands, and Judy Connors hugged Bill and patted his face. He told her that he would like to take them out to dinner. He would call them soon.

The Connors left Bill's office. He sat at his desk and read over the will to be sure it was all written correctly. This was a wonderful gift, a total surprise, nothing he ever expected or deserved. He did have considerable wealth himself. He had been able to save and accumulate as he began his practice over ten years ago. His practice was thriving; all of the cases he could take on kept him very busy. He had considered bringing in partners, but so far he hadn't done so. Perhaps now he could really look into it, and decide on a larger office also. He was content with where he lived. At this point, he wanted to stay in the condo, but one day he might build a home and find someone to love and marry again, maybe raise a family. It was hard for him to visualize himself taking care of babies, but he supposed that every man longed for a family sometimes. He was no different. His heart and mind right now were of mixed emotions.

He rang for Betty. "Please come in my office, Betty."

"Sure, boss. I'll be right there. Are you okay?"

"I'm fine. I just want you to read over the Connors will and type it up as soon as you can."

"I want to talk to you a little while. Okay, boss?"

Betty took Bill a cup of coffee and went into his office. He handed her his legal pad with the Connors will written in longhand. "Read this and tell me what you think." He drank the coffee while Betty read. She didn't look up as she read but smiled intently. When she had finished reading, she looked at Bill. "No one deserves this more than you do, boss. The Connors regard you highly. I'm elated for you. I'll get it typed immediately."

"Betty, let's go to a restaurant tomorrow night, have a glass or two of wine, maybe even go dancing. We can 'kick back' and have a little R&R, enjoy a night out on the town."

"Okay, boss, sounds like fun. I'd love to go to dinner with you."

"Good, I'll pick you up about seven. Go ahead and type this up. I'm going to call it a day. It's only three o'clock, but I need to pick up my cleaning and run by and get a pizza, maybe a few groceries. I'm going to rest tonight. I'll see you tomorrow night. I'm looking forward to it."

"So am I, Bill." She left his office, and felt like she was floating on air. Yes! Yes! She had wanted to go out with Bill forever. What should she wear? How to fix her hair? Oh, she would worry about that later. It would take her from now until four thirty to finish up here and close the office for the weekend.

Bill gathered his belongings and headed to the Ranger. He drove by Pizza Hut and got a pizza to go and ran by the cleaners and picked up shirts and suits he had there. Then he made a quick run to Food Lion to pick up a few essentials and extras for the weekend. From there he was on his way home. Tonight he was finally going to get some rest and a good night's sleep. What a day! He had been willed a fortune by some very dear friends and had made a date with his secretary. He hadn't thought of Zoa all day. Of course, there would have to be a decision made there—whether he would continue to see her or not. He would deal with that another day.

He pulled the Ranger into the garage of his condo and closed the door with the remote. He got out, unlocked the door, and began to unload his purchases and belongings.

The condo was neat and clean. His housekeeper had been by and tidied up. She always left him some wonderful baked surprise. Today there was a basket of brownies and cookies and a loaf of bread. How lucky could you be to have a good housekeeper that also baked? He put the pizza down and went to hang up his cleaning. He got his business belongings and put them on his office desk. He was ready now to get undressed and into sweats, but first, he would enjoy a few minutes in the hot tub before he ate dinner. He was so relaxed that he drifted into sleep and must have been there thirty minutes before the ringing phone woke him. He knew that he was not going to get out of the tub in time to answer, so he just leaned back and lay there with his eyes closed. For a while he knew that this was just what he needed. As a matter of fact, he planned to eat dinner and go to bed and sleep all night. He hoped that no one would interrupt his plans.

He got out of the tub, dried off, and pulled on warm sweats. He went to the kitchen, opened the pizza, cut a large slice, and poured himself a glass of wine. He ate the slice of pizza quickly and was going for a second slice when the phone rang again. He checked the caller ID and did not recognize the number, so he decided not to answer. Immediately a voice came on the answering machine, saying, "Hello, Bill, this is Carol Evans. Remember, we met at a bar association meeting a few months ago? You said we would meet some time for coffee. I was wondering if you were free on this 'thank goodness it's Friday eve.' If you are free and interested, call me on my cell phone—306-6618."

Goodness! He had forgotten about Carol. She was a very pretty attorney from a small town not far away. Her husband had died a couple of years back, and she was lonely, as he was. They had talked, and he had mentioned having coffee or dinner sometime. Carol was probably his age, but mostly he remembered how beautiful she was. He had forgotten her, and then he had met Zoa. Oh boy! Did he dare revive himself, call Carol, and go out for coffee? He thought he would at least give her a ring. He dialed the number as he sat back in his chair.

"Hi, Carol," he said when she answered.

" Hi, Bill, how are you? I wasn't sure you would be at home when I called. It's good to hear your voice. How have you been?"

"I'm fine, Carol. Everything's going well. How are you?"

Great," she said.

"I'm sorry I never did call you so we could have dinner. I've had several cases, and court dates taking a lot of my time."

"Bill, are you seeing anyone now?"

"Carol, I have been seeing someone. She isn't an attorney, but she is a very nice person."

"I'm sure she is, Bill. Are you in love with her?"

"I'm trying to sort that out, Carol. I like being with her, and she is beautiful, and she already loves me, but I've been married before, Carol, and I know feelings don't always last. My practice is first in my life right now."

"Bill, I'm glad you're honest with me, but I'd love to see you again. The time we met at the conference was brief, but we seemed to be drawn together. Do you think the chemistry between us is enough for a cup of coffee together?"

Bill laughed. "It would be nice to see you again, Carol. Tell you what: I'm already in my sweats for the evening. But I'll put a pot of coffee on, and I have some goodies my housekeeper made. Come on over and we'll talk and catch up on each other's life. I live at the Woodhaven Condos downtown, building number 12."

"Are you sure it's okay, Bill?"

"Sure it is. Come on over."

"See you shortly."

Bill hung up the phone. Well, there goes my early bedtime, he thought. He finished eating the slice of pizza, started a pot of coffee, put some brownies and cookies on a plate, and took them and two cups, saucers, and napkins into the living room. He lit the gas logs in the fireplace and lit some candles sitting on the coffee table, where he placed the cups and goodies. He put a CD on for easy listening.

The doorbell rang. He opened the door and invited Carol inside. They hugged, and Bill led her into the living room. She looked around and told him how beautiful it was and what good taste he had. He thanked her and told her it had taken him a while to get it like he wanted it. They talked about homes they liked, and he said one day he hoped to build a nice place. Right now, the condo was perfect for him, and convenient to the office. Bill went to the kitchen, brought the coffee pot in, and poured each of them a cup. He sat down next to Carol and offered her the brownies and cookies. She chose a brownie, and he a cookie, and they sat and drank their coffee and caught up on past days, their practices, and how they both were doing, he since his divorce, and she since her husband's death. They were enjoying the conversation. Bill thought how lovely she was. Her face lit up and eyes grew larger as she talked, and as she listened to Bill talk. He felt that she became engrossed in him and what he was saying. There was a longing in her eyes, a soul-searching look. He knew that tonight was not the night, but he felt he would love to get to know Carol better.

They seemed to have a lot in common, especially since both were attorneys. Carol stayed a couple of hours and then thanked him for inviting her over and rose to leave.

"Carol, I'm happy you called me and came over. I've enjoyed our visit. Let's have dinner soon. I promise I'll call this time." Carol gave him her home and office phone numbers. He walked her to the door and they hugged again. On an impulse, Bill kissed Carol. What he felt was an instant jolt, and he knew that they both wanted and needed more, but Carol pulled away and told him she had to go now. She opened the door and said, "Goodbye, Bill. I hope we'll see each other soon."

"You can count on it," he said. Bill knew that fate was providing him with several choices. He would enjoy each one.

Bill went back inside and gathered up the cups, saucers, and snacks, took them to the kitchen, and put the dishes in the dishwasher. He went back into the living room and sat down to unwind and listen to a CD. Alone with his thoughts, and a glass of wine, he wanted to sort some things out in his mind, come face to face with who he was and what he really wanted in a relationship—or did he even want a relationship right now? He knew he could not wait too long. After all, he was forty-six years old, but there was something missing in his life. He felt that he would find it soon. He was so sleepy. He dozed off in the middle of his thoughts.

When he awoke, it was twelve thirty. He rose sleepily, blew out the candles, and turned off the gas logs. He took off his sweats, put on a pajama top, and went upstairs to bed. Sleep came quickly. He slept until nine o'clock Saturday morning and just lay in bed and relaxed for a while. He didn't have anything pressing today. A little laundry to take care of, a few errands to run, and a review of a court case that would come up next week. That was all on his laptop; and of course, he had a date tonight with Betty. That should be fun. He intended to see to it that it was an extraordinary night for her. She was such an asset to him at the office, and made his days.

Leisurely, Bill rose from bed and went to the bathroom. He looked at himself in the mirror. Boy! He had slept hard. His hair was standing on end, and his eyes were swollen from slumber. He washed his face in very cold water. He turned on the shower, pulled off his pajama top, and stepped in to wake up totally. Perhaps he'd drank too much wine last night, because he felt like he had a slight hangover. He let the water run over his body, his face, and neck, and shampooed his hair. By the time he dried off, he was coming to life again.

He dressed in casuals for the day and went to the kitchen to make breakfast. He sat down at the kitchen table and enjoyed a cup of hot coffee, along with a breakfast burrito and a raspberry-filled pastry. After breakfast, he cleaned up the kitchen and put his laundry in to wash. He changed his bed and put fresh linens on. While his clothes washed, he went to his office and pulled up notes for the upcoming trial next week. He read over the notes and checked through the papers in his briefcase to be sure the information was all correct. He studied the briefs carefully, concentrating on the main points. After about an hour, he decided it was time to take a break and get the laundry folded and put away. He now had fresh underwear, socks, sweats, and pajamas for another week. He folded each piece and put them all in the chest in his bedroom.

Bill was a neat person—everything in its place, he felt. His fresh and good looks were a product of his caring attitude about himself. He laid out the clothes he would wear tonight for his date with Betty. Since they were having dinner at a nice restaurant and going dancing later, he felt that a tie and shirt and a nice sports jacket would be appropriate. He would probably remove the tie during the evening.

He dialed Betty to see if everything was still on for tonight. She didn't answer her phone, so he assumed she was out getting ready. He would give her a ring later.

Bill received a call from Bill Connors to see if their will was ready. He told Connors that he would meet him and Judy at the office. He was sure that Betty had typed it yesterday after he left the office, and notarized it also. He would check and be sure, and they could sign it. Connors told him that they were on their way to Florida and felt they needed their copy to take with them. When they arrived at the office, the will was ready, so Bill and the Connors signed it, and they took their copy. Bill filed the other copies. They said goodbye, and Bill wished them a safe and good trip. He told them to call him if they needed anything.

Bill left the office and drove downtown to do some errands. He stopped and got his hair trimmed and styled. Since his marriage to Christy, he had worn his hair longer and had grown a nice beard. It was always trimmed, but his graying hair made him appear older, although it did give him a distinguished look. Today, he had the stylist give him a new look—one that might change his life somewhat, a new image. She shaved his beard completely, covered the gray in his hair with a nice shade of golden brown with highlights, and gave it the newest style to suit his face and wonderful brown eyes. Bill was awed when he saw the look in the mirror. He felt years younger, and like a different person.

When he had walked into the salon to get his hair and beard trimmed, he had made the decision to go all the way with it. He was going all-out for his date with his secretary tonight. Then he went to get a bottle of wine to take to Betty's, and to the florist to get a dozen red roses for her. His last errand was to the grocery to get some items for the coming week. Bill most often fixed his own meals rather than eating out. He had to eat lunch out if he was in a trial. Otherwise, he skipped lunch, but he usually fixed a nice dinner if he wasn't going out. Today he bought a few rib eye steaks to grill, pasta, vegetables, ingredients for salads, some fresh fruit, rolls, cereal, milk, and sweet rolls for his breakfast. He went to the checkout and paid for his purchases. He stopped and bought a newspaper and headed to the car wash to drive through and get the Ranger cleaned up. He looked at his watch, and it was late afternoon. He drove home and unloaded his purchases, put away the food items, refrigerated the flowers, and put the bottle of wine in to chill.

He dialed Betty's number again. This time she answered on the first ring. "Hi," Bill said. "Are we still on for tonight?"

"Sure, Bill. I'm so excited. I've been getting ready all morning."

"Yes, I tried to call you and thought you might be out shopping. I'm excited too, Betty. I have a big night planned for us."

"Hey, boss, you didn't have to go to so much trouble."

"It was no trouble, and tonight I am not your boss, I am your date, and I want us both to have a grand time. Okay?"

"Okay, Bill—I'm with you."

" Okay, see you in a couple of hours."

Bill went to shower again and dress for the evening. He had taken a big step today, and he was glad he had done so. Now he showered and dressed for the evening in the clothes he had laid out earlier—gray slacks, grape-colored shirt and tie to match, and black sports jacket. He looked young and vibrant, not like his old self. He wondered how Betty would like the look. He went to the refrigerator and retrieved the bottle of wine and the roses and headed out to Betty's house.

Her home was not far from his, just a few blocks away. She lived in a cozy Victorian cottage in the historic district of town, the same section where he and Christy had lived before their divorce. As he drove through the neighborhood, he passed their old home and thought of their years together. He had given the house to her when he'd walked out of her life forever. For just a moment he wondered how she was doing. He made himself forget as he drove into Betty's driveway. He rang the doorbell, and Betty answered and invited him inside. She looked absolutely stunning in an ankle-length filmy dress, sleeveless and V-necked, almost the color of Bill's shirt, a deep grape color, with matching sandals. Her honey blond hair was pulled away from her face, and she wore lacey silver earrings. Bill had never seen her look so lovely. When she saw Bill with his new look, her mouth dropped open, and she just stood and stared at him.

"Wow! I hardly recognized you, Bill. You look ten years younger and so sexy."

"That's just the image I need—huh? Do you really like it—tell me the truth."

"I love it."

"Are you ready to go, dear?" He handed her the roses. "For you, and the wine for our nightcap."

"Thanks, that's so sweet of you." Betty got her purse, and they left to drive to Nashville, a few miles away. The Nashville restaurant Bill had chosen was the Lowe's Vanderbilt Plaza Gold Room for dinner, and later the Terrace for dancing. There was a small band playing and romantic piano music. Bill had reserved a discreet table where they could enjoy dinner and have privacy to sit and talk as long as they wished. Candlelight glowed as they were seated. Bill ordered glasses of wine, and the night began. He lifted his glass to Betty and said, "To my wonderful secretary and friend, and to this 'our' night together." He took her hand and kissed it lightly.

"Thank you," she mouthed, and for the first time Bill saw tears in her eyes. She said, "I'm just so touched by all of this."

He said, "It's for both of us. We both need this night alone." They talked and drank the wine, and soon the waiter came to take their order for dinner. Both ordered Caesar salads, grilled chicken breasts with mushrooms, and French-style green beans with almonds. They decided to split the dessert, raspberry cheese cake. Betty said, "Bill, we'll have to diet for six weeks."

He laughed. "I'll be running every day."

Betty felt so good with Bill. She saw him every day and worked closely with him, but this was different. He was so casual and at ease, and she knew she had to tell herself, 'Be still my heart. He is off-limits to you.' It would be hard, she thought, to work for him if she let herself fall for him. She knew this was just a fun evening, nothing more. Bill did not forget to tell her how pretty she looked and how he was enjoying being with her. That was Bill. They finished eating, and he paid the check. She ask to be excused, and went to freshen up. Bill slipped out also, but got back to the table before she returned. "Are you ready to move out on the Terrace for a little dancing?"

"Of course," she replied. "It's been a while, but I love to dance."

They went outside, where couples were already dancing to music played by the orchestra. They found a table. Bill removed his tie and pulled his shirt collar out over his jacket. He took Betty by the hand and led her out onto the floor. He took her in his arms as they danced to "May I Have This Dance." Bill looked so young and carefree tonight, so alive and ready to enjoy life. Of course, Betty knew that he was not completely happy with his life yet, but this was a start. He was the finest attorney around, and someday the rest would fall into place. They talked about that as they danced, and Bill felt close to Betty. He felt that it was possible that he could like her in a romantic way.

She felt good in his arms. She was a little older than he was, but how much did that matter—a few years? He looked into her eyes. They were so beautiful, so blue and clear. He pulled her closer and kissed her on the tip of her nose. She was mesmerized by him. "You know," she laughed, "I would love another glass of wine." She had to break the spell. So they went to their table and ordered. They sat and talked and talked. Then she said, "Let's go back to my house and open the bottle of wine you brought."

"Let's," he said, and so they started home.

It was close to twelve o'clock when they arrived at her place. She unlocked the door, and they went inside. She lit some candles, and he went to get the wine and uncork it. She said, "Bill, we better take it easy. We've had quite a bit to drink." He poured two more small glasses, and they toasted each other—to their most wonderful night together. "To Betty, the best secretary ever."

"To Bill, the most handsome and successful attorney in town."

He took her in his arms and kissed her, a sweet kiss, a thank you kiss, a goodnight kiss. "It was so much fun," he said. "I'll call you tomorrow and be sure you don't have a hangover."

"I'm fine," she said, "just high on the wonderful night with you."

"Sleep won't come easy, as I remember. See you Monday," he said, and she walked him to the door and stood there until he drove away.

Bill drove the short distance to his condo and pulled the Ranger into the garage. He unlocked the door and went inside. He felt wonderful about tonight. It had been a great evening with Betty. He knew she felt the same about being with him. The kiss was so sweet. He could have taken it further, but he felt it was best to be friends for now. So much was "up in the air" now with his love life, and Betty understood and wanted to be there for him. He needed her in that capacity now. Who knew about the future?

He went to undress for bed. On the spur of the moment, he dialed Betty's number. When she answered, it was like his breath was taken. "Hi, are you okay?"

"Talking to you makes everything okay," she said. "I'm so happy you called, Bill. I was thinking about the kiss. It shook me. I know it was a friendly kiss, but it felt so good, and I can't sleep."

"Hey, same here. Too much wine, you think?"

"No, I don't think so."

"Me neither. Betty, do you want to sleep with me?"

"Oh yes, yes I do, no doubt. Bill, I wonder how that would affect our working relationship. I've wanted to go out with you for so long. I dreamed of it, but never felt you would ask me out. I felt so close to you tonight, so utterly absorbed by you, and when you kissed me, I just wanted to melt in your arms. I've been dreaming about how it would be to have you make love to me."

"Let's talk for a while," he said, and they did until the wee hours.

He went over his breakup and divorce from Christy, his relationship with Zoa, and his feelings in general. He had never been so open and frank about himself. It felt good to be able to share his feelings with Betty. He told her that at this point, he didn't know what he wanted. "I know you're not a woman who would sleep with a guy and forget it. I need to have you beside me now as you are, my excellent secretary. Let's keep it that way right now. I'm going to settle down again someday. Maybe a relationship between us would work if we choose to pursue it."

Betty said, "I agree, but now we know how the other feels." They talked a little while longer, and then hung up. Betty had a hard time getting to sleep. Bill was on her mind, and in her heart . . .

Bill couldn't sleep either, so he decided to get in the Jacuzzi. It was three a.m., and to go to bed at this point would be useless. He thought of the night with Betty, what a calming, sweet presence she was.

She was a woman who understood him a lot, one who knew him and accepted him as he was. She made him want to change his life. Not his business life, but his personal life. He was going to create a plan to change, a thought process that would move him forward and leave old baggage behind. He wanted to become a new person and let go of the past. It wouldn't be easy, but he knew he could do it. Starting this morning, he was going to attend services at a local church. How long had it been since he'd been to church? Too long, he felt.

He got out of the Jacuzzi, dried himself off, and went and took a hot shower. He went to bed and set his alarm for seven, about three hours away. He was asleep within minutes. He slept peacefully and arose when the alarm went off. He made a pot of coffee and sat at the table and enjoyed a cup with a raspberry-filled pastry. Later he dressed and drove to early services at the local church. It felt good, the peace he received from worship. He vowed to return here each Sunday.

After church Bill went to O'Charley's for lunch alone. He wished Betty were here eating with him. Later he drove by his sister's home and visited with her family. It was good to just "hang out" with family, something he hadn't done in a while. He wanted to spend more time with them. He felt they needed each other. The children were young and they clung to him, so glad he was there. His sister, Rita, invited him to stay for dinner, but he declined, promising to return soon. He left and drove home, thinking on the way that he would take a nap when he got there. Somehow he felt lonely, but he would work on the case he had coming up this week. There was a lot to go over in the briefs that he'd brought home with him on Friday. Keeping busy was what he needed to do, so he went inside and went to his office to work.

Bill was up early on Monday morning. He had a sweet roll and coffee and dressed for the office. The court case he had been working on would come up this week. He felt that he was prepared but would review it again this morning and also meet with Betty to go over his appointments for the week. He had thought about some changes he might like to make in the office. He had spoken with some young attorneys who were interested in coming in as partners. He felt that two of them would be suitable for his firm. One was a friend he had known for some time, who had been practicing law for three years. In the back of his mind, he also thought of Carol Evans, but was not sure how that would work out. This morning he would go over these considerations with Betty. He was ready to move on—new beginnings.

He arrived at the office in good spirits. He felt great. Betty was already there, had made coffee, and was working in her office. He walked to her door and said, "Good morning, how are you?"

"Great!" she answered. "And you?"

"I'm fine," he said. "I had a fabulous weekend. By the way, I want you to know that Saturday was great. I enjoyed our date and had a wonderful time. It was fun being with you."

"I feel the same," she said. They chatted for a while, and he asked her to come into his office when she had a minute. " I'll be there ASAP," she said. "Want a cup of coffee?"

"Sure," he said.

Betty finished what she was working on, took her pad and pen and two cups of coffee on a tray, and went into Bill's office. She set the tray down and sat in a chair next to his desk. They began to discuss upcoming appointments; he brought up his ideas and asked for her ideas and input. As they chatted, the phone rang. Betty went to her office to answer it. It was for Bill, so she transferred the call to his phone. She heard Bill gasp and say, "Oh no! I can't believe this. When and where did it happen? I'll be there as soon as I can get a flight. I'll bring my secretary to help, if she can get away. Okay. I'll be there soon. Goodbye."

Betty walked back into Bill's office. He had his head down on his desk. Betty asked, "Bill, what is it? What is wrong?" He raised his head, and there were tears in his eyes. He said, "Betty, this is a terrible tragedy. Bill and Judy Connor were killed in an airplane crash last night. They were on their way to their home in Florida. Bill was flying his Cessna N20. I have to fly down to Fort Myers to bring them back. Do you think you could fly with me and help? We'll be gone a couple of days, so my appointments will have to be cancelled, the office closed, and we need reservations."

Betty walked over and put her arms around Bill and hugged him. "I'm so sorry, Bill. They were such nice people, and really cared for you."

"You know, Betty, they were like family. I can't believe this has happened. They called me Saturday and asked if the will was ready, and I told them that you had typed it and notarized it on Friday. They asked if I could meet them at the office and let them sign the will and give them their copies. I knew you had it all ready, so I met them, and they signed it, took their copies, and left mine. They told me they were going to Florida and wanted everything in order before they left. Both were in good spirits and looked great. They were still so enthused about leaving me all of their estate. I feel so bad. Do you have a Tylenol? My head is throbbing."

"Yes, I'll get you one, and a Coke."

Betty left his office. Bill went to the bathroom and was sick. He washed his face, walked to Betty's office, and got the Coke and Tylenol, hoping it would help his head and cure the nausea he felt.

Betty was on the phone making reservations and canceling appointments for Bill. As she finished, she saw that Bill was not well. "Bill, lay back in this chair, and I'll wash your face." He did, and Betty washed his face so gently. Tears flowed from both of their eyes. He looked at Betty so intently. She kissed him so gently, and hugged him tight. "Bill, it will be okay. Just relax, and your headache and nausea will pass. I have airplane reservations at five o'clock. Do you want me to go to the condo and pack you a bag?"

"Betty, I need to go home, get a shower, and try to feel better. We have several hours until flight time. Do what you need to do, and close the office. Call the florist and have a wreath put on our door. I'll have to make arrangements when we return."

"Don't think about that right now." Bill lay where he was. Betty stood next to him and continued to comfort him.

He felt so good with her. He began to feel better now, and became aroused. He pulled Betty to him and kissed her full on the mouth. It was a different kiss than the one he'd given her on their date over the weekend. "Thank you so much for being here with me."

She returned his kiss and said, "I'll be with you through this, and I'm glad to be here." They both felt something they had never felt before, a comfort and peace in each other, and a strong connecting of souls. Bill felt well enough to get up from the chair, go back to his office, and get ready to leave. Betty followed him to be sure he was okay and to discuss their final plans.

Bill said, "I think we should leave about three thirty. I'll be packed by then and ready to go."

Betty said, "Why don't I come by your condo, pick you up, and drive you to the airport? That way, you can rest and relax a little before the flight."

"That sounds great," he said. "I think we both'll be able to relax on the flight."

"Okay, see you in a little while," she said.

Betty called the florist and ordered a wreath for the office door. She asked them to please wait a couple of days before hanging it. She turned all the lights out and checked everything, then locked the doors and left the office.

Betty was a strong person. Her strength would see her through this tragic event, and she would walk tall and be there in every way for Bill. She felt so wonderful inside when she thought of him. Together they would make it through this. Bill would have a lot to do, and she would help him. She knew that was what he wanted.

Betty drove home as soon as she closed the office. She packed a bag for their trip to Florida. She took a quick shower, dressed in a fresh pantsuit, rested a little while, and was ready to leave by three fifteen. She drove the short distance to Bill's condo, giving him a call that she was on her way. He told her he would be waiting outside.

She pulled into his driveway, and when she saw him, her heart skipped a beat. She wondered how it would be to be married to Bill Roth and go to bed with him, spend her days with him, and make him happy. He smiled when he saw her. He got in the car and put his bag in the back seat. "I'm so glad you're driving us. I took a shower and tried to relax and feel better, and I do feel a little better. Betty, this is such a horrible thing. I can hardly get it out of my mind."

"Bill, it'll be okay. I'll be with you, and together we'll make it."

He took her hand and kissed it. "I don't know what I'd do without you in my life." The bond that they both felt at that moment bound their lives together in a way that they both would understand some time later.

The flight to Fort Myers was uneventful and smooth. Bill and Betty relaxed, slept part of the way, and talked the rest. Betty had called ahead and made arrangements to rent a car, and also hotel accommodations. They would be staying in adjoining rooms at the Radisson. First on the agenda would be to go to local authorities and try to find out the details of the Connors' airplane crash. Then, if permission was given, Bill would arrange to have Bill and Judy Connors' bodies flown back to Tennessee. Bill thought, barring any problems, it would take two or three days to get the bodies released. Bill and Betty had talked about a service for the Connors, and since their wishes were not known, they decided to seek out some of Bill and Judy's friends to talk to. They discussed a graveside service and would make the decision later. Bill wanted to honor his friends in a special, but quiet way because that was the way they lived their lives.

He thought back to the first time he had met them, and to the most recent appointment they'd made with him to write their will. Even though Bill knew the Connors fairly well, he was totally shocked when they wanted to leave him everything they had, and he never ever thought they would die so quickly. As he thought about it, the queasiness returned, but this time, he wept. "Bill," Betty said, "please don't do this. You'll make yourself sick again." She took his hand. He put his arm around her and held her close to him. The stewardess announced that the plane was landing, and seatbelts should be fastened. Betty and Bill fastened theirs as the plane came down. They went directly to the airport restaurant and got snacks and drinks. Then, they went to get the car they had arranged to rent.

Bill made a phone call to the local authorities to let them know they had arrived. They told him they were waiting to talk to him. So Bill and Betty drove to the Fort Myers courthouse, where they met with police, the sheriff, highway patrol officers, a judge, and the coroner. They told them about the crash and when and where it had happened, just a few miles from town.

The Connors had owned their home here for several years and flew down periodically for R&R. They were well known by the locals. The judge spoke to Bill and Betty, describing to them what the authorities felt had happened just as Bill Connors prepared to land his Cessna N20. The plane had been cleared for landing, but for some unknown reason, it started to descend too fast and clipped trees as it crashed to the ground just outside of town. There were no calls to the control tower. The plane just went down and caught fire as it crashed. Some rescuers rushed to the scene and were able to extinguish the fire, but both Bill and Betty Connors were already dead. "Their bodies were burned some, but not completely," the judge stated. He asked Bill's permission to have an autopsy conducted to see if perhaps Bill Connors had some medical problem that had caused the crash. He said, "I'm sorry to have to put you through this, but I know that you want to know what happened, as we all do."

"Of course," Bill said. "I want to help and cooperate in any way. Betty, my secretary, and I will stay as long as it takes to get answers." Bill spoke to the judge privately about the Connors coming to him recently to have a will made and their leaving all of their estate to him. The judge said, "I know, Bill, they regarded you highly, as their attorney and friend. They spoke of you often like a son. They said they trusted you entirely."

Bill, with tears in his eyes, told the judge. "When I wrote the will, I was overwhelmed when they told me they wanted to leave everything to me. I couldn't believe it, and I surely never ever thought they would die so soon. They told me that they felt they were in good health, but one never knew, so that was why they wanted to get the will done at once. Betty stayed that evening, typed, and notarized their will. We prepared to call them back to sign it on Monday, but on Saturday I received a call at home from Bill to see if the will was ready to sign. I told him to meet me at the office, which is what he and Judy did. They signed the wills and got their copies. They were leaving town to come down here and wanted everything in order. They seemed well and happy."

"Listen, Bill, you mustn't worry and fret over this. As soon as the autopsies are complete, I'll release the bodies to you to take back to Tennessee for burial. Some of us here who knew the Connors well will want to come back for the service. I realize this is a terrible blow to you. If there's anything we can do for you, let us know. Why don't you and Betty go get some rest, have dinner, and go visit the Connors home? It's a lovely place located near the water. I have the keys, as we took the baggage and personal belongings that were left."

"You know, Judge Parker, I'm too wrought to pursue that tonight. I'll call you tomorrow if that's okay, and perhaps we can go there together."

"I understand, Bill, and please call me tomorrow. This'll be settled in a couple of days, and you'll know and understand more and can go from there. Please take care, and thank you for coming and for being a wonderful friend to Bill and Judy. You'll understand their feeling for you as you uncover the assets they've bequeathed you. I don't know you well, Bill, but what the Connors felt you are means you must be tops."

"Thank you sir," Bill said." I'll see you tomorrow."

As Bill left the judge's office, he spotted Betty waiting for him in the foyer. Together they left the courthouse and drove back to the hotel where they were staying. Bill told Betty on the drive over, "Let's rest and shower and find a nice place to have dinner."

"Good idea," she said. "Are you okay?"

"No, I'm really not okay. This is a horrendous shock, but I'll get through it with you by my side. Listen, I need to call Rita, my sister. She knows nothing about this, and I need to let her know where we are. I may not give her all the details now, but just let her know why I'm here."

Betty said, "Okay. I'll go take a shower, rest a little while, and give you a chance to make any calls you need to make. Knock on the door or call if you need me."

"Okay, dear," he said. " I may need you." He grinned. Betty knew that he did need her, and she him, but somehow that would work out; soon, she hoped.

Bill made the call to his sister. She could tell by his voice just how devastated he was, even though she knew there were things that Bill wasn't saying. "I'll call you later, sis," he said, "and tell you all the details. It feels good to hear your voice, Rita."

"I love you, Bill," she said. Rita and her children were Bill's only family. Bill's parents had passed away several years ago. His dad had been an attorney also, as had his dad before him. Bill and Rita had grown up in a loving atmosphere, and it was times like now that he missed family. He had been on his own for a long time, but he yearned for the family he had once known. Perhaps that was why the Connors were drawn to Bill. Perhaps he was the son they longed for, and they the parents he missed.

Bill hung up his cell phone and went to shower. He thought of Betty in the suite adjoining his. She had traveled all the way here with him, standing by, waiting to see how she could help him and what would ease his sadness. He felt a need to talk to her right now, so he put on a terry robe and called her on his cell phone. She answered at once. "Hi, you didn't expect me to call so soon, did you? Were you resting?"

"Actually, I was almost asleep. I had a shower, and just came in and laid down."

"I'd like to talk, if you're up to it. I just feel that I want to spend some time with you."

"Come on over. I'm in my robe, if that's okay."

"Hey, I am to, so let's just wear them." Betty opened the door that connected their suites. Bill came in with a casual terry robe on. They were dressed almost alike. Betty's heart raced as she looked at him. She knew that she was here to comfort him, but it didn't stop her female desires from surfacing.

"Would you like a cup of coffee or some juice? There's a basket of fruit in the foyer," she said.

"A cup of coffee sounds good," he said.

"How about if I fix each of us a cup?"

"Sure, okay." Bill went to the tiny kitchen and made them both a cup of coffee. He brought them to the foyer–sitting area that contained a sofa and a table. He set the cups on the table. They sat side by side as Bill spoke. "I want to thank you for coming here with me and supporting me during this difficult time. It means more than you can possibly know. I've never felt the warmth and concern from anyone as I have felt it from you during this whole experience. You've been my secretary for a few years, a superb one I must add, but I've never felt the connection I feel to you right now. That you . . . you truly care about me."

They had been sitting close, and he was looking into her eyes, and at that moment they each felt something in their hearts that would soon change their lives. Bill slowly took Betty in his arms and kissed her, lovingly, passionately, and seductively. This time he did not stop. They did not speak. Each kiss became deeper and more inviting and drew them closer together, and they both knew that it was the beginning of something wonderful, something neither had ever felt before or would ever feel again. Betty's deepest desire was to give herself to this man she had secretly loved ever since the day she'd walked into his office. She knew him so well. Knew what he had gone hrough and who he was. Knew she could blot out all of his past and love him forever. Knew that together they would make a wonderful team, both in business, and in life.

Bill knew also. He felt the desire, the passion, run through him like electricity, and this wasn't the first time.

He had been fighting it a long time, he knew. He knew that this was more than the desire for a beautiful woman. It was the connection of one soul to another, and he wanted this woman to be with him forever and ever. She would erase his past and lead him into a heavenly future. Together they would soar to heights unknown, as man and wife, and lovers, and in life.

Bill took Betty in his arms, lifted her and took her through the doors that connected their suites, to his bed, where he slowly and passionately removed their robes and made love to her as he had never made love to another woman in his entire life. Their lovemaking soared, each giving the other a pleasure never unleashed before, and as they reached their climax, they became one in body and spirit. Bill held Betty so close and looked into her clear blue eyes. "Marry me," he said. "I love you and want you with me forever."

"Yes, I'll marry you, my love. I want to spend the rest of my life with you just like this."

Bill and Betty stayed in his bed the rest of the night, reaching heights of passion and love beyond anything either had ever experienced or imagined. They made plans for their wedding as soon as they could get back home and things were settled. They discussed having Betty attain her law degree and join him in his practice. She was already a paralegal and it wouldn't take her long. "Bill, I want to have your baby real soon."

"Okay," he said, "that comes first. I want that too." Bill wanted what Betty wanted, and she wanted what would make him happy. Whatever would satisfy the other, they wanted. Bill felt as if his heart would jump from his chest with joy. Betty lay in his arms as they fell asleep, so content and satisfied.

Bill awoke first the next morning. He felt like a new man. As if he had been transformed and left one life to start another. He could see now, and knew exactly what he wanted and in what direction he was going. All of his thoughts and feeling, desires and hopes, included this woman lying beside him. Somehow he felt he had known this a while but had not recognized it or let his heart feel the depth of it. How foolish he had been wasting so much time.

Betty awoke, and Bill said, "Good morning, sleepy head. I love you. It's a new day. Let's shower and find some food. Do you realize we haven't eaten since the airport snack when we arrived yesterday?"

"I haven't missed the food," she said. "You've filled my very being." He kissed her passionately. "Whoa!" she said. "We better get our showers, or we'll never get going." Betty got out of bed, put her robe on, and went to her suite to shower and dress, giving Bill the opportunity to have the privacy to do the same, even though they both agreed it would be wonderful to shower together. They would do that later.

As soon as they were both dressed, they found a nice restaurant nearby to have breakfast. They each ordered hot coffee and a big breakfast, saying that if they weren't able to eat for a while, it wouldn't matter. Betty told Bill she would find something else to do while he rode with the judge out to the Connors' home this morning. Betty felt it would be best for him, but Bill wanted her to come with them. "Are you sure?" she asked.

"I'm positive," he said. "I'll give Judge Shockley a call and tell him we'll pick him up or meet him there."

"Bill, are you anxious about seeing the home?"

"I would have been before, but now I feel better about everything, and I know I have you by my side."

"I've always been by your side, Bill."

"I know you have, but now we're together in everything. It feels so good, my love."

"Me to," she responded.

"I'll have to make lots of decisions now, and you'll be with me to help me."

Bill dialed the judge and asked if he wanted them to pick him up. The judge told Bill that he would meet them there in an hour. He gave Bill directions to the house. While they waited, they sat and talked about their wedding. They both agreed it would be small. As a matter of fact, both thought it would be fun to get married in a wedding chapel in the mountains of Tennessee, and they could honeymoon there also. They discussed where they would live and decided it didn't matter so much as long as they were together, but Bill said he wanted to build a nice place for them someday.

Betty was excited as they talked of plans to enlarge his law office and bring in new partners. Neither talked about the assets Bill would inherit from the Connors. They just could not think about that now.

As time drew near, they drove according to the judge's directions from downtown about two miles to the bay area. The Connors' house was close to the beach and was a magnificent white clapboard home with beautiful sea-colored shutters and a wrap-around porch. It was a two-story structure with a balcony overlooking the bay, and an in-ground swimming pool and spa. There was a cabin-sized cruiser boat in back under an aluminum canopy. Bill and Betty pulled in at the back of the house just as the judge arrived and parked next to them.

"This is a wonderful place, isn't it, Bill?" the judge asked as he shook hands with both of them.

"It sure is, sir."

"The Connors must have loved coming here. They spent many happy hours in Fort Myers, Bill, and entertained their friends here with dinners and gatherings. I was here with my wife many times for cookouts, swims, and dinners. This will all be yours now, Bill. I hope you plan to keep and enjoy it."

"I hope to be able to do that, sir." Then Bill told the judge of his and Betty's plans to get married. "She's been by my side as my secretary and friend for a few years. We discovered that we love each other and feel so close since we've been here. Well, actually, I asked her out on a date recently, and I think we both began to realize that something was happening between us." Bill reached for Betty and pulled her close.

The judge smiled, "That's fantastic. Now you'll have a law partner and a wife."

"We're so excited, and in love," Betty said.

"It shows," the judge said. "Let's let you two see the inside of this beautiful home." He took the key and unlocked the door. They walked inside and felt the presence of the Connors. Everything reminded Bill of his friends. All was so warm and inviting, so restful and relaxing, so unpretentious and peaceful. It was a legacy to who these folks were.

After the judge had shown Bill and Betty around, he told them that the coroner had called him this morning and said that the autopsies would be completed by noon. "We'll meet with you about one o'clock, Bill, and go over the reports. I believe you'll be able to take the bodies back to Tennessee by tomorrow. I'll help you make flight plans and arrangements as soon as we get the reports. Have you thought of a service?"

"You know, sir, there was no mention of their wishes when I wrote the will for them. They never talked about that sort of thing."

The judge said, "They didn't talk to me about it either, but once Bill mentioned that they had bought mausoleum crypts for their burial there in Tennessee. Do you think they would have wanted a graveside service? I can get in touch with their pastor at the church they attended. Bill and Betty, you two go ahead and plan the service. Some of their friends here will want to fly back for it. We'll talk more after the report today. I have to get back to the courthouse. I'll see you both at one o'clock in my office. Here's the key to the house. Keep it. It's yours now. Stay here a while and look around. This'll be a marvelous vacation home for you and Betty. The Connors would want you to enjoy it. See you in a while."

The judge left. Bill took Betty's hand and said. "Let's walk." They each pulled off their shoes and headed down the beach. They walked for a while without speaking. They just soaked in the sea breeze and enjoyed the sound of the waves hitting on the shore and the sea gulls flying about. Bill stopped, pulled Betty into his arms, and kissed her a long passionate kiss that left them both reeling. "If you weren't here with me right now, I couldn't make it through this time. There are so many decisions to make. I can't even think what to do next."

"Bill, it'll all work our, and be okay. The decisions you make will be the right ones. You've always done things that way, and I'll be with you to help any way I can. How soon do you think we can be married? I want that more than anything."

"As soon as things are settled. I tell you what: Let's lock up the house and drive back to the hotel and stay until time for the meeting. I want to be with you again as we were last night."

"I'm ready, Bill, let's go." They ran barefoot back to the house, locked the doors, and drove like crazy back to the hotel.

Bill unlocked the door to his suite, and they both were undressing as they went to his bed. He could not wait to make love to Betty again as they had the night before. He kissed her and touched her, and the excitement they felt could not be contained. She responded to his every move, brought him to pleasures he had never ever experienced, and took him to heights from which he did not want to descend. They made it last and last until neither could hold off any longer—then they became one again and held each other so tight that neither could move. "Don't move, love. Stay locked in my arms like this forever." They kissed and kissed, and the passion rose again, and it was like new all over again. They simply could not get enough of each other, and Bill knew without a doubt that this was beyond anything he had ever experienced in his life. He gave himself to this woman he had fallen in love with, and he never wanted to remember the past again. He was a new man.

Bill and Betty barely had time to shower and dress before going back to the courthouse. They arrived just as the judge and others gathered for the autopsy hearing. They took a seat as the coroner began to read the report. He said that Bill Connors had experienced a sudden massive coronary heart seizure just as the airplane he was piloting began to descend. There was nothing that could have been done. He had died instantly. It was probably a moment of terror and trauma for Judy Connors before the plane crashed, and she died on impact. There was no doubt whatsoever as to the cause of the crash. The plane had been in perfect condition, and the weather and landing conditions had been excellent. The plane would have burned had some witnesses not seen the crash and extinguished the flames. Judy Connors had received some burns to her arms and legs. Bill Connors had also, and they both had broken bones but were recognizable. The coroner signed the report and passed it to the other officials to sign.

He released the Connors' bodies to Bill and had him sign the papers. Bill had not seen the Connors, and he did not wish to now, but as their attorney and friend he had to make proper identification.

Betty walked with Bill, and the judge took both of their arms and walked with them to the coroner's lab. Bill, who truly was a strong man, wept as the sheets were pulled back. He could not stop. Betty put her arm around Bill to console him, and the judge took both of their arms and led them back outside. He told them that he had made reservations and arrangements for them to fly back to Tennessee tomorrow if they would be ready to leave. Bill told the judge that he had spoken with the Connors' pastor and the funeral home. They would meet them at the airport. The judge told Bill that he and the others would fly up for the memorial service. Bill told him that he would call as soon as arrangements were made, and they would be able to land their private plane in town. "I'll have transportation waiting for you."

"That sounds good. Thanks so much for coming here and for being a wonderful counselor and friend to the Connors. They seemed more like my family. There'll be a deep void in my heart and life for a long, long time."

Bill and Betty left the courthouse and drove back to the house by the bay that Bill would inherit. They parked the car and went inside. They walked through the house and looked at the lovely but simple furnishings. It was as if the Connors were welcoming them, saying, "Come, stay a while, and visit with us." Bill was overcome with sorrow and grief for his friends, and tears rolled from his eyes. He walked out onto the porch and looked out to sea. Betty did not disturb him or interfere. He needed this time alone to grieve. He sat in one of the lovely wicker chairs until he felt relief from some of the pain he felt, and then walked back inside where Betty was waiting. She had found sodas and fixings for sandwiches, and chips. She had fixed two plates at the table in the kitchen. He walked over, took Betty in his arms, and held her against him. "I love you," he whispered. "I love you so very much."

"I know," she said, "and I love you, Bill."

They sat together at the table, ate, and talked. Bill asked Betty what she thought he should do with this house. He wasn't sure that he could keep all of the houses. "I'm not sure we would come here that much," he said.

Betty said, "I think you should think it over a while. You don't have to make the decision right now. You're too grieved."

"You're right," he said. "I just feel so sad here now."

"I know," she said. "Let's clean up the dishes, lock everything up, and go back to the hotel. You can ask the judge to check on things until you can decide what you want to do with this house. Let's chill out a little, drive around the town, and then go back and pack and enjoy the rest of the time together."

Betty cleaned up the dishes while Bill locked up the house. They left and drove around town before going back to the hotel. They each went to their own suite to pack their bags and spend a few moments in thoughts and relaxation.

Bill knew that he did not want to be away from Betty for long. Goodness! He had come to love this woman so much. He could not wait until they were married and could be together all the time. Wouldn't those who knew him be surprised to learn about him settling down again? He felt so good about everything.

The door between their suites was open, so he walked into Betty's. She was in her bedroom packing her bag. He walked in and they were together at once in each others arms, kissing and touching and ready to make love again. This time on her bed, passionately, exploring each other, as their hearts and souls joined together and beat as one. Each knew that here, in this town, at this sad time, something wonderful had bound their lives together forever. They no longer thought as individuals but as one person.

Bill and Betty were packed and ready to leave Fort Myers by nine o'clock the next morning. Their flight was leaving at ten, and the rental car had to be turned in. The judge came to see them off, and a funeral car brought the

Connors' bodies and put them on the large jet. Bill became so sad, and wept as the two draped coffins were loaded onto the plane. Betty and the judge also shed tears as they tried to comfort Bill. Bill hoped he slept all the way back to Tennessee, because he felt so numb. The judge shook hands with both of them as they boarded the plane. "Take care and we'll see you soon," he said.

The flight to Tennessee took a couple of hours. Bill and Betty both slept all the way. The plane landed at twelve thirty.

A funeral car was at the airport to take the Connors' bodies back to their hometown. Their pastor, Dr. Albert Smith, was there to console Bill and Betty and to talk to them about funeral arrangements. Bill told Dr. Smith that they would meet with him at the funeral home later in the day.

They picked up Betty's car from the airport parking lot and headed home. Betty drove, and they talked about the office for the first time since they'd left town a couple of days ago. "Let's go there, check messages, and see how things are going. It feels like we've been gone a long time. I'm anxious to get back to work. Are you in love?"

"Yes, I am, but things are different now. Will you still feel the same about me being your secretary?"

"No, love, not the same, but I want you to still be my secretary until we're married. Then you can decide what you want to do." He took her hand and kissed it, and as they drove into town, they went straight to the William T. Roth law office, and it was wonderful to be home.

A funeral wreath was on the door, and numerous messages were on the voice mail, so Betty went to work retrieving the messages and answering them, while Bill walked into his office and closed the door. He sat in silence thinking of the past few days, the changes that had taken place in his life, and those that would begin to take place. He had cases coming up in court soon. He was up on those and had prepared or begun to prepare for them. The memorial service for the Connors would likely take place on Friday, a few days away. After that, he would talk to some contractors about enlarging the office here. He would begin to consider new partners, and if Betty wanted, he would bring her in as a partner as soon as she finished her law degree. Above all, he wanted them to be married as soon as possible. He thought two weeks or less would be time enough to prepare. That thought really got him excited. A weekend in the mountains, and now they could honeymoon in the cabin the Connors had left him.

Betty buzzed Bill. "Honey, are you okay?"

"Yes, sweetheart. I'm just sitting here thinking and planning. Do you think we can plan our wedding and get married in two weeks?"

"Yes, I believe that's plenty of time," she laughed. "We'll talk about it in a little while. I've answered all the messages, Bill. Your appointment with Dr. Smith at the funeral home is at two o'clock. I'll stay here at the office and get some work done while you're there. I think we should call Judge Shockley in Fort Myers as soon as plans and arrangements are complete. I think a memorial graveside service will be appropriate at the mausoleum on Friday. Dr. Smith will conduct the service, and the judge and others should deliver the eulogy."

"I don't feel that I can speak, Betty. It's just too much for me. After the service, do you think you can help me with a small reception for some of the Connors' friends at my condo? It'd be very small, quiet, and personal."

"Of course I will, Bill. Just tell me what you want. I want you with me always. It's done. I'm yours."

Betty hung up the phone and went back to work. Bill slipped into a jacket, took Betty's car, and drove to the funeral home. Plans were finalized for Friday, and Bill called the judge in Florida. "There are six of us flying up," he said. "We'll fly in there about noon on Friday."

"Fine," Bill said. "There'll be a car at the airport to pick you all up, and directions to my office. We'll all go to the funeral home together."

"That sounds good, Bill. We'll see you on Friday."

"Oh, sir, I would like for you and some of the others to deliver the eulogy. Do you think you could do that?"

"Of course we will, Bill."

"Also, there'll be a small gathering of their friends at my condo after the service."

"We'll be there for that also, Bill. Please stay in contact with me after this is over."

"I plan to do that, sir."

Bill headed back to the office. Betty was still at work. "I've made calls to the Connors' friends here and told them about the service and reception on Friday."

"Thanks, love. Now can we talk. I have some things to run by you."

"Sure. I'll come in your office in a few minutes."

Bill went into his office, sat at his desk, and pulled up information he had stored there concerning his first legal case coming up on Monday. He was anxious to get to work, but he was also checking his schedule to see if he'd be free in two weeks so that he and Betty could get married. His calendar was clear for the weekend of September 15. He would talk to Betty about it when she came in. Betty came in shortly, bringing each of them a tall glass of iced tea. She walked over to his desk and kissed him. She knew it was not professional, but she knew he wanted her to, and there was no one there but the two of them.

"I love you," he said. "I want to talk to you about the weekend of September 15 for our wedding."

"It's fine, Bill. I could be ready by tomorrow."

"Me too," he said. "But there are other things going on, and a trial coming up on Monday. We can call the wedding chapel in Gatlinburg and set things in motion."

"That sounds wonderful, honey."

"Do you have family you want to invite?"

"I'd like to invite Rachel, my sister, and her husband, Wayne. That's all the family I have left."

"Okay," he said. "We'll ask them, and I'll invite Rita and Carl and their children, Sara and Sam. That way, we'll have family with us. We can make reservations for them, and we'll all have dinner and a reception at a nice restaurant after the wedding. Then, you and I can honeymoon Saturday and Sunday at the Connors' chateau."

"That sounds so exciting and wonderful, Bill. I can hardly wait."

"Me either," he said. "I'll go ahead and get it set up and make the reservations."

"Also, I need to talk to you about the flowers and food for the funeral and reception on Friday."

"Just simple flowers and food will be fine."

"How many are we planning on, Bill?"

"Six are coming from Florida, plus about twenty from here, you and I included."

"Will trays be okay? Maybe a meat tray, fruit and cheese, some chicken and shrimp, and a pastry tray."

"Large trays will cover it all, and coffee, tea, some wine for drinks."

"I'll take care of it, Bill. Angela, your housekeeper, and I will set it up at the condo."

"Thank you, my love."

"Do you want to live at the condo after we're married until we decide where we want to live?"

"That sounds great, Bill. I am so looking forward to our being together all the time."

"I am to," he said.

On Friday Judge Shockley and other friends of the Connors flew into town. Bill had arranged for two cars to meet them and drive them to his office. He was there to greet them. Betty had been at Bill's condo with Angela, his housekeeper, preparing for the reception after the service. They had everything ready. Betty would join Bill at the mausoleum for the service. Bill and the others drove to the funeral home to meet and speak with Dr. Smith, the Connors' pastor, and other friends gathered to follow the entourage back to the mausoleum where the service would be held. Bill shook hands with everyone and introduced them to the Florida group. No one except the judge knew that Bill would be the beneficiary of the Connors' estate, but they all knew he was their attorney.

Dr. Smith asked that they all gather around the coffins as he said a prayer. Betty had ordered beautiful red rose sprays for the coffins. Bill thought how proud he was of her, and how much he loved her as he looked at them. Tears stung his eyes, and he blinked. The pastor said a few words and then prayed an inspiring prayer. The entourage of around twenty then followed the funeral car to the mausoleum. Betty was there to join Bill for the service.

There were chairs set up, and three pretty floral wreaths on stands. Dr. Smith read passages from Psalms and Ecclesiastes, read a poem he had written, and talked of his association with Bill and Judy Connors and how much their lives had meant to him. Judge Shockley spoke of the tragedy that had taken the Connors' lives, and how he had come to know and love them in Florida. He spoke of Bill Roth, and how the Connors loved him as their friend and attorney. Bill could not contain the tears. Betty took his hand. Others from Florida spoke, telling great stories of their association with the Connors. At the end of the service, a friend of the Connors sang, "God Be with You Till We Meet Again." Dr. Smith prayed and the Connors' coffins were put inside of crypts in the mausoleum. Bill sat and watched and saw that his friends were taken care of, and then he asked the others there to follow him and

Betty to his condo in town for the reception they had prepared. It was a sad time, but a tribute in a quiet way to two lovely people who had impacted the lives of those who had gathered.

Bill and Betty saw that everyone had food and drink as they listened to stories and talked of their friends' lives well lived.

Bill rode with the judge and others back to the airport to say goodbye. He ask the judge to take the key to the house in Fort Myers and keep a watch on it for him until things were settled and he could make a decision about it. The judge told him he was glad to oblige and would be in touch soon.

Betty drove out to the airport to pick Bill up as soon as she and Angela had stored the food that was left and straightened up Bill's condo. He was so glad to see her, and said, "Let's stay at the condo tonight, love. I'm so tired, and I know you are to, but I want us to be together tonight, and its Friday. The office is closed. Who knows about the weekend?"

"I'm ready to go where you want to go, darling. We should keep this respectful, you know, until we're married. No one knows about 'us' here except that I'm your secretary."

They'll know soon, love, Bill thought. *They'll know soon.*

The weekend went by fast. Bill and Betty were together—at his condo and at her house. They rested, made love often, and talked of their wedding and of their future together. They talked about the office and what role she wanted there after the wedding. Betty wanted to please Bill, and so she let him take the lead in the plans.

"I know I can never find another secretary that could compare to you, so if you want to keep that job and take courses to get your law degree, we'll bring you in as my partner, and maybe one more person to round out the firm. I believe we could pull in more cases that way. We really don't have to push ourselves so hard, as all of the money and property I receive from the Connors' estate will see us through our lives many times over, but I love the law, the practice of it. I want to continue working until I'm old enough to retire. It won't be my first priority, as in the past, but I want to keep on working at it. Who knows, maybe we'll have a son who'll take over one day."

Betty grinned and said, "That would be awesome, darling, but don't forget, neither of us are real young. At this stage it's still possible, and maybe probable." Neither was really concerned. They just wanted to enjoy each day together and let the future and fate take care of themselves. The future for them was to be one—one heart, one soul, one life.

Bill went to the condo to brief himself on the early morning case on Monday. Betty went to her home to make plans for her new life, and her wedding. They would live this way for two weeks, respectfully, but they would see each other and be together any time they wished outside the office. It would be hard, but it would work. They would let others know of their plans gradually.

On Monday, both Bill and Betty were at the office early. Betty stopped on her way in for donuts for them. Bill's client for the early morning trial was with Bill when she arrived. She went directly to her office, made fresh coffee, began to retrieve computer e-mail messages and phone voice mail, and began her morning routine.

Bill was defending a young man this morning whose wife was suing him for divorce. There were two children, six and seven years old, and a custody battle was very evident. Bill was coaxing his client not to "lose his cool" and jeopardize the case. The couple had been married eight years. The wife was involved with another man. The young man, Steve Lewis, wanted custody of his children. Bill was confident that he could convince the judge that Steve would be the right parent to raise the boys.

Bill buzzed Betty's office just because he wanted to hear her voice. "Hi," he said. "How are you this morning? Do you have any coffee?"

"Yes," she said, "and donuts too."

"Could you bring in a couple of cups of coffee and some donuts? We can use them about now. It's about forty five minutes until trial time."

"I'll bring them in shortly, love," she whispered. He got the message and couldn't wait to see her. It had been twelve long hours.

Betty brought the coffee and donuts into Bill's office on a tray. She spoke to Steve Lewis and asked Bill if there was anything else they needed. He looked at her so intensely. "That's all, right now. I'll probably be out of the office until lunch. I've asked some contractors to come in and look around to see about changing some things. Will you make notes, and we'll go over them later."

"Sure, Mr. Roth. I hope things go well for you today in court, Steve," she said, and closed the door to Bill's office.

Bill continued talking with Steve Lewis as they drank their coffee and ate the donuts. He briefed him on the questions he would be asked and told him that he had to let him do the talking, no matter how mad or upset he became. "The calmer you are, the better things will go in the court room. Think of the boys and you'll be fine."

"I'll try my best, Mr. Roth."

"Remember, I'm here to help you, Steve." So, at five minutes to nine, Bill and Steve walked to the courthouse. Bill was in good spirits and was prepared to win this case.

Betty continued working on Monday morning routines. Calls came through for appointments with Bill. The contractors came in and walked through the building, measuring and looking to see what changes could be made. Betty took notes so she could fill Bill in on the details. Some of the changes would definitely update the office and perk things up. She thought Bill would like the changes suggested. The update would definitely give the Roth firm a new image.

Bill gave Betty a quick call on his cell phone when the judge called a recess at the courthouse. He asked her to order lunch for him and Steve Lewis. It seemed the trial and hearing would last all day. Softly, he whispered, "I love you."

She said, "I miss you being here."

"I know," he said. "I hope we can get away early if the trial ends."

"I'll have everything caught up here," she promised.

"Good. We'll be there in another hour or so for lunch. Will you please order sub sandwiches, chips, and sodas for us?"

"Okay, love. Oh! Bill, I think you'll be pleased with the changes the contractors have recommended."

"Good. We'll talk about it later. I have to go now. I'll see you in a little bit."

Betty sat and daydreamed a little while as Bill hung up the phone. She felt so connected to him now, so in love with him. He gave her goose bumps just talking to her on the phone. She had always loved receiving his calls from the road as he traveled, or from courthouses where he was in trials. It was different now. She never thought, even though she hoped that they would fall in love, that he would love her so deeply as she felt his love now, and that they would marry soon. She was still his secretary, and it was hard for her to "be cool" around him. Well, she had errands to run and some typing to do, so the daydreaming had to end. She would lock the office, go to the bank and the post office, and pick up the subs for Bill and his client. Betty ran the errands, returned to the office, and put Bill and Steve's lunch on a tray on Bill's desk. She had a salad and iced tea at her desk while she worked and answered the phone.

Bill and Steve came in, went directly to Bill's office, and closed the door. Betty had a feeling that things were not going as well in court as Bill had hoped. He spent the entire lunch hour with his client and went back to court without saying a word to Betty. She knew he was upset. Bill worked on lots of divorce cases, but where small children were involved, he became emotionally involved, and wanted the best outcome for the little ones. In his heart, he knew that Steve Lewis was the best parent for these children, but things must not be going so well, Betty felt. There was nothing she could do for him at this point.

She had typing to finish and the morning mail to process. Keeping busy was what she needed to do now. She was so engrossed in what she was doing that she did not hear the door open and someone enter the office. As long as she had worked for Bill, she had never been afraid to be here alone. It had just never entered her mind.

As she looked up from her work, she was staring at the barrel of a gun being pointed directly at her. There was no time to scream or dial 911, no panic button to push. Holding the gun was a scraggly looking young man starring at her wildly, disheveled and shaken. "Listen, lady, I'll use this on you without regret unless you give me all the money you have in this office." Betty had been to the bank earlier and deposited all the money she kept for office purposes. She probably had two hundred dollars in her purse, and maybe fifty dollars in the petty cash box. She wondered if that amount would keep this young thug from taking her life.

"There isn't much here," she said, "but I'll give you what I have."

"How much?" he demanded.

"Two hundred fifty dollars," she said.

"Hand it over," he said. "And you better not call the police or anyone until I've had time to get out of here, or you'll be very sorry." Betty calmly took the cash from her purse and the petty cash box and handed it to this wild-looking young man, who crammed it into one jacket pocket and the gun in the other and ran out the door. Betty ran and locked the front and back doors and then sat down at her desk and wept. She called the police and reported the robbery. She described the man, in his early twenties, she felt. They told her that they would start looking and that someone would be right over to talk to her. She asked them to please knock on the front door, since it was locked. "I was threatened with a gun," she told them. "Bill Roth is in court, and I'm here alone. Please hurry."

"We'll be right there," and they were. When they arrived, they had already caught the man, and they returned the two hundred fifty dollars.

Betty was so happy, but she kept the doors locked until Bill returned from the courthouse at close to four o'clock. When she told him the story, he couldn't believe it. To think someone would have the nerve to pull a prank like that right here on the town square. He took her in his office and held her close to him. "I won't let this happen again. We'll have to take some security precautions to be sure the office is safe while I'm away. You could have been killed." He hugged her, held her, and kissed her so gently. "I love you so much," he said. "Are you okay?"

"I'm fine," she said, "and I got the money back."

He grinned. "Your life is more important to me than any money."

"I'm reluctant to ask," she said, "but how did Steve's divorce trial go?"

"They get the divorce, and joint custody of the boys. Steve won't have to pay her alimony, but he will pay joint child support, and got their home. He feels that she will marry this other guy soon, who he says is very well-off. Steve is such a nice guy. I knew how bad he wanted those boys. I really talked for it, but the judge felt they needed to be with both parents. Steve promised me he would try to accept, make the best of, and enjoy the time he had with them. You know, Betty, I'm so glad that Christy and I didn't have children."

"I am too, Bill."

"Let's finish up here and head over to the condo, what do you say?"

"That sounds wonderful. I think I hear the Jacuzzi calling our name."

Bill and Betty closed the office and each drove their own vehicle to his condo. Betty stopped by her house to pick up extra clothes and a casserole that she had put together the night before. She drove over to Bill's and parked in his driveway. He was waiting for her and was so glad to at last have her to himself alone. He had already filled the large Jacuzzi with water and had candles burning all around the tub. He had on a pair of swim trunks and a terry robe. Betty put the casserole in the oven and set it on low temperature for them to enjoy later. She had on a two-piece swimsuit under a short dress, which she started to unzip. Bill walked over to her and took the dress off, and it was as if they both would explode with passion, as they held each other, kissed over and over, and made up for time they had lost being away from each other. "I missed you so much," he said. "You are the light of my life, a beacon for me, a haven of love. Forgive me for not recognizing that a long time ago."

"You are my dream come true at last," she said. He took her hand and led her to the Jacuzzi, and they got into the relaxing water and stayed there together, loving and planning their wedding that would take place very soon. Life was just beginning for them, and they were so happy.

On Tuesday Bill had a hearing before the probate judge concerning the Connors' will and estate. Since Bill was the beneficiary of the will, he felt that he needed counsel with him, so he asked a lawyer friend, Eric Cooke, to represent him before the judge.

At this point, no one in town knew that Bill had inherited considerable wealth and real estate. The judge read the will and discussed it with Bill and his representative. Everything seemed in order, they agreed. As the amount of the estate was tallied, it was estimated that it would exceed well over one hundred million dollars. Bill could not believe the extent of what he would receive.

He would have his tax consultant help him understand it all. It was a lot of money, but he planned to use it wisely, as the Connors would have wished. The estate would not be completely settled for three months, so that would give him time to make some decisions. The Connors never offered any advice about what he should do with the three houses they were leaving him. He felt it would be a wise thing to sell their home in town and keep the chalet in Tennessee and the beach house in Florida. He wasn't sure how much time he and Betty could spend in Florida, but he knew that they could use the chalet often for weekend getaways.

The judge asked Eric Cooke representative to print and publish ads in the paper in case there were debts against the estate. Everything would be paid first. He dismissed the two of them, and they went back to Bill's office, where they discussed the details. Eric said, "Bill, do you realize that you are a very wealthy man? You won't have to ever work again."

"Eric, you know me better than that. I wouldn't be happy sitting around. Besides, who would face you in court?"

"You're right. I can't see you not practicing law."

They both laughed. "You know, Eric, I haven't told you my latest news."

"What? You're already rich and don't need all of this money."

"Don't be funny, man. You know better than that. Seriously: I'm getting married again."

"Shaa! Who, and when? I thought you were through with that phase and planned to be a bachelor the rest of your life."

"I did think that way after the divorce, but that was before I fell in love and found my soul mate. To answer your question, Who? Betty Davis, my secretary. When? Next weekend in Gatlinburg. Eric, she is the love of my life, and I know it this time. I want this more than anything, and I plan to be with her forever."

"When did this all come about? The last I heard, it was Zoa Britton, and many others before her. Are you sure this is right, Bill, my friend?"

"It started on a date. I took her out just because she was my secretary and friend. We both felt a connection that night, but when the Connors died suddenly, she stepped in and stayed with me, consoling me and helping me through a very difficult time. I knew then that she's a person that I can trust and depend on, and she makes me happy, and we're in love. Enough said."

"Congratulations, Bill! You are one lucky guy—inheriting a fortune and finding the love of your life."

"I didn't find her, she was already right here with me."

"I'm happy for you. What can I get you for a wedding present?"

"What about if you join me in the Roth law firm as a partner?"

"You're kidding me."

"No, I'm offering you a partnership."

"Give me a little time to think it over, Bill."

"Take all the time you need, my friend. You're still representing me through this probate, though."

"Of course. I can't back out now. It's a piece of cake—be settled without any problems. You know that already. Guess I better go. I have a date for dinner. I'm just having fun, though, not serious like you. I'm kidding, of course. Give me a ring before next weekend. I wish you every happiness, Bill."

"Thanks," Bill replied, "I am very happy." Bill sat at his desk and thought as Eric left. He had known Eric a long time, and he knew that he would be an asset to the firm. He hoped that he would come aboard. Bill buzzed Betty when Eric had gone. "Hi, sweetheart. Why don't you come in here and let's talk?"

"Sure. I'll be right in."

She brought her pad and pencil ready to take dictation, but Bill just wanted a moment alone with her. He got up from his desk, took her in his arms, and kissed her, once, twice, three times. "Hey! We're still at work, you know, but I'm not complaining at all."

"Nor I," he said. "You look and feel so good."

"So do you," she replied. They both sat down, and Bill filled her in on what had gone on today. "Sounds great," she said. "When will Eric let you know about joining the firm?"

"Sometime after our wedding, I think. Speaking of the wedding, I was thinking we need to send out announcements to our friends and clients. We don't need this to be a complete shock to everyone."

"I had some announcements printed. Bill, for you to look at and approve."

"Good! I thought perhaps you would." Betty went to her office and brought the printed announcements for Bill to read. "They're perfect. Simple and pretty," he said.

"I'll get them in the mail the first of next week before we leave. I've called our families to let them know of the reservations and time of the wedding. It'll be at twelve o'clock on Friday at the Garden Wedding Chapel. The flowers and music and clergy will be provided by the chapel. The dinner and reception will be at the Marriott, where we all will be staying. I have my dress and clothes ready. Does all that sound okay to you?"

"Will it be okay if I wear a suit?" he asked.

"Of course, it isn't formal. I feel the simpler, the better. I'm just so excited, I could cry."

"So am I, but let's just bask in the wonderful moment. No tears, just happiness."

The rest of the week went smoothly. Bill wrote several wills for clients. Every time, he thought of his friends, and it made him sad, but grateful for their generosity to him. He saw other clients and worked on cases that would be coming up in the future. He went over the plans with Betty that the contractors had suggested for changes to the office. He wasn't sure exactly how and where they would work while the renovations were going on. There was an empty building nearby that they might be able to use. He called to check on it and told the owner he would let him know soon.

On Friday Bill and Betty decided to leave town for the weekend. It was a getaway for both of them before their wedding week, and Bill felt they could be alone, talk, and not have to deal with townspeople. They went to a lake house over in Kentucky owned by a friend of Bill's. It was a lovely cabin next to the water and was equipped with everything they would need for an enjoyable stay. There was a magnificent view from the deck, a large wood-burning fireplace, and a Jacuzzi. It was like a pre-honeymoon cottage, and both felt so romantic.

All Bill wanted to do was to be with Betty his love, and tell and show her how much she meant to him. They made love often and slept in each other's arms. They hiked through the woods and fields, taking in all of nature. They cooked breakfasts together and drove to the nearest town for fish dinners. They rode horses and had twilight hot dog and marshmallow roasts. It was like being kids again, except they were much older. They were so happy together. They each felt they would explode.

The weekend ended too quickly and they were sad to see it end, but they knew it would only be a few days until they would be man and wife. On the way home from Kentucky they stopped at a quaint country inn and had dinner. They talked about the coming week and some things they needed to finish before Thursday. They had decided to drive to the mountains early Thursday morning and go by to see the chateau that the Connors had left Bill. Bill wanted them to spend their honeymoon there, but he felt that it would be nice to check into a room at the Marriott on Thursday with the rest of their family that was driving up for the wedding. Betty agreed with him that it would be the thing to do. He took her hands in his and looked into her eyes. "Do you know how incredibly happy I am?"

"Yes, I do," she said. "I feel it in my heart and see it in those dancing brown eyes. Did you know that is what captivated me the first time I met you, those piercing brown eyes, and each time I came into your office, I felt the intensity of those eyes."

"I never knew that. You should have given me a clue," he laughed. "I'm so happy that I'll be able to look into those eyes and get lost for the rest of my life."

"So am I," he said as he kissed her. They didn't want to part when they drove into town, but they had agreed that each would stay at home until the wedding, at least most of the time. The announcements would go out tomorrow, and others would begin to understand their togetherness. "I'll miss you, love," Bill said, as he left Betty at her house. "I'll see you in the morning. I love you."

"I love you to." She waved to him as he drove away.

Bill was at the office early on Monday. He had work to do that would keep him occupied all morning. He was writing two wills, representing a young couple in an adoption case in court, talking with another client who was getting a divorce, and going to look over the building they would use as an office while renovations were made to their office. It was close by, so no problem there.

Betty didn't come in until nine o'clock. That was unusual for her, but Bill wasn't too alarmed. She knocked on his door when she arrived, which she seldom did. As she came in, he could see that she was pale and not feeling well. "Close the door, love," he said. "What's wrong?"

"Bill, I'm sick. I must have eaten something at the inn yesterday on the way home." She began to cry. Bill got up from his desk and walked over and put his arms around her.

"It's okay. We don't have an appointment for an hour. Go back home and lie down. I can handle everything here."

"No, you can't, Bill. There's too much to do this morning, and the phones will be ringing off the wall. I think the nausea will pass after a while, and I'll be okay."

"Do you think so?" He grinned. He already knew what was wrong with his dearly beloved. She was going to have his child.

"Oh, my goodness," she said. "You know."

"Of course I know," he laughed. "I'm not entirely innocent. How long have you known?" he asked.

"About a month, but this is the first time I've been sick."

"I'm happy," he said.

"I am too," she said. "This is what we both wanted, and the clock was ticking." Bill held her close and told her that this was the happiest day of his life. She said, "I hope it's a boy, a son, for you, to carry on your name and your legacy as an attorney."

"Whatever it is, we'll love and cherish it as we do each other," he said as he smiled again.

Betty felt better, so she went to work, and Bill saw his first client in his office. The rest of the day went smoothly.

They both felt like they were floating on a cloud. In the afternoon, when it was time to go home, Bill took Betty to his condo. "You'll stay with me from now on. I'll take care of you and see that you're okay."

"Bill, let's not tell others about the baby for a while. They'll know in a few months, but we'll be married, and it won't be such a shock."

"Whatever you want, my love, we'll do."

"I'm fifty years old, my darling. You're only forty six. We're a bit old to be having our first child, but I pledge to you, the best for us is yet to be."

"I already know that," Bill said.

Tuesday and Wednesday went by fast. They both finished the work that needed to be done. Bill decided that they would rent the office close by temporarily until their office was updated. He got a crew to move their equipment, and others to start work on the building while they were out of town for the wedding. He didn't want Betty to have to worry about anything. He was assured that it would be finished in a month; six weeks at the most. Their temporary office would be set up and ready for business when they returned.

Bill spoke with Eric Cooke on Wednesday. Eric told him he would like to join him as a partner in his firm, but it would be a few months before he could close his own office. Bill told him that would be fine, there was no rush.

He told him of the renovations he was having done. "I guess you're getting excited about now, man!"

"Yes, I am. We can hardly wait until tomorrow and Friday. We'll be leaving town early and driving up. The wedding will be at twelve o'clock on Friday. Some of our family is joining us."

"Again, I say, Bill, I am so happy for you. I believe this is the right thing for you this time."

"Believe me, Eric, I know it is, without a doubt."

Bill wished he could tell his friend that he was going to be a father, but he could not right now. Everyone would know in a few months; and sometime around June, Betty would give birth to their child.

He said good bye to Eric and hung up the phone. He sat there and thought about Betty and the baby. He would take the best of care of her and see that she got the rest and nutrition she needed. If he had to hire a new secretary, he would until the baby was born, or even longer. He would worry about her until the time came. He knew now that his life was different, and he was glad. His heart was so full of love for his wife-to-be, and their child.

Bill and Betty packed their bags and clothes in the Ranger and headed out of town around nine o'clock on Thursday morning. They planned to stop along the way for breakfast and get into Gatlinburg around noon. They were very eager to see the Connors' lovely chateau. All of the fall foliage would be in color, so they could do some sightseeing before the others arrived. Betty was feeling good now, so she would not give her pregnancy away. She so much wanted to wait until after the wedding to tell the others. She knew Bill did too. As they drove into Gatlinburg, the scenery was so beautiful, it took their breath away. The winding road leading up to the Connors' chateau was picturesque. The cabin itself was a dream getaway. A two-story structure of wood and glass with a porch on the second story, it overlooked the mountains around and the town below. There was a Jacuzzi in the master suite that was huge. A deck and pool was at the back of the ground floor. That floor also housed three bedrooms, two full baths, plus a kitchen and den with a fireplace. All Bill and Betty could do was to stare in awe. It was furnished simply, nothing fancy at all, but the chateau and surroundings were spectacular. "This is just where we need to be," Bill said.

Betty hugged him and said, "I wish we could stay here forever."

"This will be our getaway. We'll definitely come here often." They looked around for a while, and then locked up and headed to the Marriott to check in and pay for the rooms for their family. There were three suites reserved, and Betty's and Bill's sisters and families were already unloading their bags. They were all so glad to see each other and be together. "Have you all had lunch?" Bill asked. No one had, so they all went to O'Charley's for lunch, and then walked around the town sightseeing. They talked about the wedding, and Betty told them that everyone should meet at the chapel around eleven. "Let's all meet at nine for the continental breakfast, those who can get up that early. Then we'll have time to get dressed, and over to the chapel."

Rachel, Betty's sister, would be her matron of honor; and Carl, Bill's brother-in-law, would be his best man. Bill's niece and nephew would act as flower girl and ring bearer.

Everyone was so excited and ready. They sat and talked until late. This was the first time Bill had met Betty's sister and her husband, even though Betty already knew Rita and Carl, and their children. They all got along so well, welcomed each other as family, and vowed to get together a lot in the future. They said their good nights and went to their suites.

Everyone was up early on Friday, even though sleepy headed. They met at the buffet for breakfast. The children slept in, and Rita took their breakfast to the room for them.

Bill and Betty were so hyper; they took a long walk after breakfast. As soon as they returned, they showered and began to dress for their wedding. Betty's dress was a simple straight dress with a short jacket in a beautiful shade of taupe and gold. She wore her hair up with pearl and gold dangle earrings. Her shoes were gold sandals. Bill, always so handsome, wore a dark navy suit with a gold shirt, and a taupe, navy, and gold tie. They were such a beautiful couple together, and the love they felt and shared showed in their eyes and on their faces.

"Are you ready to go, my love?" Bill asked. "I can hardly wait. I wish we could go directly to the chateau."

"I do too," Betty said. "But we'll have a good time at the dinner and reception with our families. Then we'll be free for the weekend."

They drove to the Garden Wedding Chapel and met their families. The chapel was decorated with beautiful arrangements of wedding flowers and burning candles. There was a bridal bouquet of cream-colored roses and baby's breath, and in the center a tiny box that contained a diamond heart necklace. It was inscribed, TO BETTY, WITH ALL OF MY LOVE FOREVER, BILL. As he presented her the bouquet, tears brimmed Betty's eyes. Then he placed the necklace around her neck.

The music began. Songs they both loved were played, including "May I Have This Dance for the Rest of My Life." The minister took his place, the attendants walked in, and Betty and Bill came in together and stood side by side as they looked deep into each other's eyes. They took their vows and exchanged rings, and they each said a few words that came from their heart. No one knew but the two of them that there was a tiny heart joining theirs on this their wedding day.

Bill took Betty in his arms and kissed her after they were pronounced man and wife. "I love you so much," he whispered. She grinned and kissed him again. Music played as they walked out, and continued as they chatted with the family. They all left and drove back to the Marriott, where a private dinner and reception had been prepared for them. A photographer snapped lots of pictures, and a scrumptious candlelight dinner was served. There was a three-tiered wedding cake, champagne punch, and chocolate-covered strawberries set up on a lighted buffet table.

Bill and Betty cut the cake after dinner, and each fed the other a piece while the family snapped pictures. Music was played for dancing. They took a few turns around the floor before they were ready to say goodbye as they were leaving for their honeymoon. They thanked each one for coming this far to be with them on this special day. The family thanked Bill for his generosity in providing lodging and meals for them. He said, "We wanted you all here with us, and we were glad to take care of it. Stay the weekend, and enjoy." The children asked if they could go with them to the chateau. "No, you can't, but I tell you what. We'll all go up there together sometime, or you can use the place anytime you wish."

"Sounds great," everyone agreed.

Bill and Betty left their families and drove up the mountain to their honeymoon hideaway. On the drive, Bill said, "Are you okay, darling? Are you tired?"

"I'm fine, sweetheart. I feel great, and I'm so happy. I want to be with you now."

They got out of the Ranger, took their bags, and went to the second-story suite, which had a king-size bed. Bill undressed as Betty went to the bathroom and undressed. She put on a beautiful lace gown she had purchased especially for this day. She knew that Bill would remove it as soon as she walked in, and he did, slowly, as he kissed her and took her in his arms to their bed. They made love on and off all night. They had made love many times since their trip to Florida, when in the middle of a tragedy they'd discovered what true happiness was with each other. Today was the climax of that happiness and the beginning of a new life for them. They slept until noon on Saturday, got up and had a sweet roll and hot coffee, went back to bed, and stayed the rest of the day, making love and sleeping until evening. They got in the Jacuzzi for a while. Bill drove down into town and brought back enough food to last them until they would go home the next day. It was a perfect honeymoon and a perfect beginning to their marriage.

They rose early on Sunday and had a light breakfast as they made plans to return here as soon as they had some free time. Betty talked with Bill about working on her law degree. "I could go to class a couple of nights a week, and by the time our baby is due, I'd be ready to take my bar exam. Bill, I could be a lot of help to you at the office."

"You're already my right hand, love, but I'm not sure about you pushing yourself so hard now. You know law school is not easy. I'm not discouraging you. I want you to get your degree, but now the baby is on its way, and I don't want you to take on too much. As a matter of fact, I was thinking of getting you some help."

"You know I can handle the office. I don't need help."

"Okay. We'll see, and remember, the decision about law school is yours. If you feel up to it, I'll support and help you."

"You're right, darling, I may be dreaming too big right now."

"You and our baby are the most important things to me, but I do want to continue to work as I am doing."

"Okay, you got it, but if you feel bad at all, you let me know. Have you seen a doctor yet?"

"No, not yet."

"Well, Monday we'll get you an appointment."

They spent the rest of the morning enjoying the chateau and its surroundings. In late afternoon they packed their bags and left for home.

They were glad to be back in town, and went straight to the condo to unload their bags and get settled in. They had talked, and decided to live here for the time being. Betty would keep her house also. She loved the cottage, and had it furnished nicely with antiques, and all of her clothes were still there. They would make decisions later about their living quarters. Bill wanted to build a nice home for them in the near future, especially now since the baby was on its way. They were so excited about the baby; it would be hard to not tell others for a while.

Betty and Bill decided to ride downtown to check on their office and see if everything was set up for business in the temporary building. They were amazed at what the crew had accomplished while they were away. Desks, filing cabinets, and phones were all in place, and William T. Roth III — Attorney was written on the door. Drapes and blinds and a few pictures added the finishing touch. They were ready for business on Monday.

They drove by Betty's house, and she got a few clothes for the coming week. They stopped and got a pizza and enjoyed it. Bill said, "I want you to rest, get in the Jacuzzi, whatever you feel like doing. I'm going to work on the laptop for a while and refresh myself on cases coming up, and then I'll join you in the Jacuzzi."

"That sounds wonderful, darling." She kissed Bill and said, "I'm so happy I'm your wife."

"So am I, my love." He felt so content now, so peaceful with her here with him, as if it had always been this way.

Things went well at the new office on Monday. They received plants and flowers and notes and cards of congratulations. Everyone was happy for them. Betty stayed busy answering the phones. One client sent a large basket of fruit and a bottle of champagne.

Bill was in court early in a divorce case. Betty stayed busy on Monday morning routines. She felt good. Bill told her to decide on a doctor that she wanted to see and make an appointment that morning. She really didn't want to go to a local doctor, so she called one in a nearby town and made an appointment for Wednesday afternoon. Bill would go with her, as he would be appointment free then.

Betty called the law school in a nearby town to discuss her interests in obtaining her degree. She wanted to know just how long it would take her to finish, with the experience she had in Bill's law office. They told her it would take six months to a year attending night school. The more she thought about it, the more she wanted to join Bill as a partner. She would discuss it with him again. A lot depended on what the doctor told her. She knew at fifty years old, and this being her first child, there was a lot that could go wrong. She felt that she was healthy, but she had to take it easy because her greatest desire was to give Bill a son.

He came back to the office after court, and she filled him in on what was going on. He loved all of the gifts they had received and couldn't wait to sample the fruit and champagne. "Let's take it home tonight."

"That's a good idea."

She told him about the appointment with the gynecologist on Wednesday. "I'm going with you," he said.

"I had hoped you would. I made it with a doctor in a town nearby."

"That's okay, as long as there's a hospital where you can deliver the baby."

"There is a nice hospital," she said, "and it won't take long to get there."

They finished up for the day and went home to the condo. Each got out of work clothes and into sweats. Bill helped Betty make dinner and clean up afterward. Then they got in the Jacuzzi and relaxed before bed. They later showered together, and Bill gave Betty a massage which led to passion and lovemaking for an hour or so. These times together each night was what they both loved and cherished.

They were ready to get up early and go back to the office on Wednesday. The time for the appointment with her doctor was at three o'clock, so Betty and Bill closed the office early and drove the few miles to Dr. David Sims's office.

After introducing himself to them and talking with them in his office for a while, Dr. Sims took Betty to do a thorough examination of her. He told her that everything seemed fine. He felt that she was in good health, and was about two months pregnant. The baby would be born in late May, around the 25th. He did think she should have a C-section, rather than natural childbirth, because of her age. "You should not have any problems as far as I can see, unless something unforeseen happens, and I don't expect that. Just take it easy, don't push yourself, and you'll be fine. We'll give you vitamins to take, and you should eat a good, well-balanced diet and get as much rest as possible. I will want to see you once a month until you are six months, and then every two weeks; and the last month, every week. I would like you to keep your weight down as much as possible. The less you gain, the easier it will be." Betty asked about going to night school to pursue her law degree. "I don't think you should do that right now. It would be too much, with your work at the office."

She understood. "How soon do you think it will be until I show? We haven't told anyone yet about the baby."

"It should be in about two more months. About the first of January, you should be able to tell." He called Bill back in and talked to both of them. "I'll be available anytime you need me. Just call if you have questions or problems." They both felt good about him. Betty told Bill that she was disappointed about law school, but she would pursue that later. "Just listen to the doctor, and you'll be fine, love."

A couple of months passed, and it was time to settle the Connors' estate. Bill and his counsel, Eric Cooke, went before the judge in early December. All of the assets, stocks, and real estate had been transferred to Bill, and he began to grasp the astronomical amount of it. His advisor and tax consultant met with him to advise and assist him in the investment to his greatest advantage. In the end Bill decided to keep the Connors cabin and Florida home and sell their home in town. He decided to use the money to build a nice home for Betty and himself. He had his advisor set up two scholarship endowments to a local college in the Connors' name. He planned to use part of the money to help others, and he gave a nice donation to the Connors' church. He bought himself a new SUV to use for travel to other towns for trials. The rest of the money and assets would be used as needed for them to enjoy. After the estate was settled, Bill was relieved. He made a call to his friend Judge Shockley in Fort Myers and had a long conversation.

Bill and Betty continued business as usual during the next few weeks. Their old office renovations were completed, and they moved back in close to Christmas. They now had beautiful, larger offices and a reception area where Betty decided to work at a round desk. Some antique pieces were brought in, and new leather chairs were used at different points with mirrors, and their favorite art work. They were pleased with the end result, and glad to be back at home.

They enjoyed a nice Christmas together and got together with all of their families on Christmas Eve. Most of all, they celebrated their love for each other, and the new baby that would be coming. They told their families about the baby, and everyone was so excited, especially Bill's niece and nephew.

Sometime in January, Betty had a sonogram, and they found out the baby would be a boy. They both were thrilled. Betty began to show, so everyone learned about the baby and were extremely happy for them.

Bill continued working on as many cases as he could take on. He found time to be with Betty, his love, and he was never happier.

In early spring, he hired contractors to start to build a house for them. It was a lovely two-story colonial style home built on a hill on some land Bill owned not far from town. There were lots of rooms and of course a nursery for their baby. A huge deck, pool, and Jacuzzi were in back where they could enjoy their free time. The house was completed in May. Bill hired a decorator to come in to help them decide on colors, drapes, and carpets. As soon as everything was ready, Bill had movers move their possessions out to the house. He closed the condo, and put a FOR SALE sign outside. Betty also sold her beloved cottage home and moved her treasured antiques to the new house. Bill loved antiques also, so their home was a blend of their choices.

Betty had gained twenty-five pounds during her pregnancy. It was close to time for her to deliver the baby. She still worked at the office with Bill. He was in court a lot, so he needed her as he always had. He called as often as possible to check on her, and came back to the office as soon as court was over. At their new home, he watched over her and wouldn't let her do any work. She began to feel bad as the time grew near. She didn't understand because she had felt so good most of the time during her pregnancy. At her last doctor's appointment, she had swelling in her feet, and legs, hands, and face. The doctor was concerned and told her that they would do the C-section next week. "I want you to check into the hospital on Sunday, and on Monday, we'll deliver your baby. Get as much rest as possible."

Bill was so concerned about Betty. He knew that he should have hired a new secretary and let her stay at home, but she wouldn't hear of it. "I can't train anyone now, Bill."

"Okay, its fine. I just want you to stay at home and rest in bed until Sunday. I'll take the rest of the week off and stay with you." So Betty did as Bill asked. She was too tired and felt too bad to argue. He stayed with her, massaging her back and comforting and consoling her. He made tea and light meals for her and packed her bag for the trip to the hospital. They talked about the baby and how happy they were.

"My heart is so full of love for you and our baby, " Bill said. "The happiness you have brought me is beyond anything I have ever received or deserved. This baby is the completion of our love." Betty fell asleep as Bill spoke. He was scared. Was there something going wrong now that the baby was due? Oh Lord, he hoped not. He closed his eyes and said a prayer: *Please Lord; take care of Betty, and our baby. She has filled my heart with so much joy, and I love her so much.*

Bill helped Betty shower and dress on Sunday and drove her to the hospital. He checked her in, and they put her in a wheelchair to take her to the maternity ward. Bill kissed her as she left. Her blood pressure was high, and she was still swollen, but the nurses did not seem to be too concerned. Bill called Dr. Sims and told him about Betty's condition. He said, "I'll be right there." When he got to the hospital, he called his assistant in to check Betty. They decided to go ahead and do the C-section right then. Bill paced the floor. What on earth was wrong? She had seemed so healthy, and he'd let her continue to work. He should have known better. What would he do if something happened to his love, his soul mate? It had taken him forever to find this happiness. He couldn't bear to think of life without her.

The doctors came out and told Bill he had a fine healthy son, a baby boy. "Betty did not survive, Bill. The swelling she had came from a condition known as congestive heart failure. It would have taken her life eventually, but carrying the baby sped the process. It didn't show up before. Bill, I am so very sorry."

Bill just stood in shock and wept. Why did this happen? How could he go on without her?

"Bill, you have your son. Do you want to see him?"

"Yes, of course I do," and so he followed the doctors to the nursery, where they handed him a bundle that contained his tiny son, who looked just like him, with piercing brown eyes and curly brown hair. WILLIAM T. ROTH IV—Tracey Roth, who he knew someday would take over his practice, would be just like both his mom and his dad, and would carry in his heart the love that they felt for each other and for him.

Printed in the United States
95796LV00005B/7/A

9 781434 333452